I0641041

Anonymous

Memoir of Frank Russell Firth

Vol. 1

Anonymous

Memoir of Frank Russell Firth
Vol. 1

ISBN/EAN: 9783337345976

Printed in Europe, USA, Canada, Australia, Japan

Cover: Foto ©Raphael Reischuk / pixelio.de

More available books at **www.hansebooks.com**

F.N. Frith.

MEMOIR

OF

FRANK RUSSELL FIRTH.

"Blessed are the pure in heart, for they shall see God." — *Matt. v.*

"But Wisdom is the gray hair unto men, and an unspotted life is old age."
— *Wisdom of Solomon, iv.*

BOSTON:

LEE AND SHEPARD.

1873.

FAME is the spur that the clear spirit doth raise
    (That last infirmity of noble minds)
To scorn delights and live laborious days ;
    But the fair guerdon, when we hope to find,
And think to burst out into sudden blaze,
        Comes the blind Fury with the abhorred shears,
            And slits the thin-spun life,
                But not the praise.
        .   .   .   .

And hears the unexpressive nuptial song,
In the blest kingdoms meek of joy and love.
    There entertain him all the saints above,
In solemn troops and sweet societies,
    That sing, and, singing, in their glory move.
And wipe the tears forever from his eyes.
                        — *Milton*.

        .   .   .   What is excellent,
        As God lives, is permanent ;
        Hearts are dust, hearts' loves remain ;
        Hearts' love will meet thee again.
                        — *Emerson*

MEMOIR.

FRANK RUSSELL FIRTH was born in Clappville (now Rochdale), a village in the southern part of the town of Leicester, Massachusetts, on the 26th of May, 1847. His father, Abraham Firth (born in Leicester, England), was then station-agent of the Western Railway at that place. His mother, Maria Louisa Firth, was from Charlton, an adjoining town, her family name being Russell.

For a few years, Frank was an only child; and being claimed by both his grandmothers as an only grandson, he was the centre of a great deal of love and admiration, and also the object of much anxiety, as his health was very delicate. His early life did not differ greatly from that of other children, and the incidents which follow are related as characteristic rather than remarkable.

By way of punishment for small misdemeanors, his mother tried the plan of shutting him in a closet. One day the little fellow was missed. After a fruitless search had been made, he emerged from his prison, and calmly said, using the name by which he was in the habit of calling himself, " Tub-er-tay naughty. Had to shut him in the closet." He was a strict disciplinarian for himself, often coming to his mother to report small sins of which she could not otherwise have known. With his clear eye and manly ways he seemed the impersonation of truth.

His active brain and fingers were always employed. At home, he often shared his mother's household occupations, beside learning, under her guidance, his first lessons from books. He was happiest, however, with his father at the station. His earliest knowledge of figures he gained perched on a high stool in the office, peering into the great freight-books. The trains had a strong fascination for him, and he numbered among his friends many of the brakemen upon them.

When he was eight years old, he began to be very useful to his father, who, in addition to his railway duties, kept flour and grain for sale in the " granary " near by. Frank used to go to Worcester with envelopes buttoned inside his jacket, containing hundreds of dollars, which sums he was to place in the bank. He is still remembered by the bank officers as their youngest depositor. His railway experience really began at this time, and he already had visions of a future when he should " run a railroad."

He would amuse himself, while riding in the cars, by counting the rails as he passed over them. When his father went away, he would mount a stool to sell the tickets, and his little hand would be raised to give the signals to the freight conductors to stop or to move on. He also made entries on the cash and order books, as well as a record of all sales on account.

Through the meadow behind his father's house ran a little brook, across which Frank built a dam, and in due time had many water-wheels in working order. The gate for shutting off the water was rather frail; a shower would cause a rush sufficient to carry it away; so it was not an unusual thing for the family to be awakened at night by the noise of the wheel, when the millwright (then aged eight) would get up to attend to it.

He also took to literary labors, and the result was, "The Clappville Herald, published weekly, by F. R. Firth, two cents a copy, $1.00 per annum." The paper was in manuscript, and made up of selections copied by its "publisher." Its political sentiments are shown by the following extract, found in a copy still extant : —

"ALPHABET OF SLAVERY.

" A is an African, torn from his home;
B is a Bloodhound, to catch all that roam," etc.

When he was between nine and ten years old he began to attend the village school. Exhibition day came, and Frank rose to speak his piece. He had chosen Barham's famous " Misadventures at Margate." He began : —

" I was in Margate last July; I walked upon the pier;
I saw a little vulgar boy; I said, ' What make you here ? ' "

The audience were not destined to hear the rest. The embarrassment of having so many eyes fixed upon him was too much ; he could not go on. He had no intention, however, of being discouraged. At the next exhibition he put forth all his strength of will, and spoke the "Charge of the Light Brigade" with great success. Later, he took part often in public school exercises ; but he was never at his ease on such occasions, as they were little to his taste.

In 1857, his father removed to Worcester, to be agent

there of the Boston and Worcester Railway. During the next four years, Frank was quite absorbed in his school. He also was a constant attendant at the Sunday school of the Church of the Unity (Unitarian), and he awakened in both his teacher and the minister (Rev. Mr. Shippen) an undoubting faith in his character and ability, as well as an affectionate interest, which never afterward lost sight of him.

At this time he developed a great taste for arithmetical calculation, constantly doing long sums mentally. He would beg his friends to tell him how old they were, and when told, would, in an incredibly short time, give their ages in minutes. In the same manner he would reduce miles to barleycorns, or gallons to gills.

During a fever which he had at this time, his mind constantly recurred to such problems, to the great alarm of the family.

Frank and several of his cousins usually passed the summer at his grandfather Russell's, in Charlton. With one of them he engaged in mimic scientific explorations or practical experiments, — digging artesian wells, blasting rocks, drilling holes in search of emery, or hunting up arrowheads and pottery on Indian Hill. When the first Atlantic cable was completed, they manufactured pitch-pine torches, and in the evening Frank instituted a procession, formed of his cousins and his sister, who was ever an admiring follower where he led.

He had another faithful admirer in his grandmother, who always believed in whatever he did. In after years her pride and affection never faltered, nor did he ever fail in the love and reverence which were her due.

His grandfather, though a farmer, has always had mechanical tastes, and has on his place a blacksmith's shop and a carpenter's bench, at both of which Frank passed many busy hours.

Near the blacksmith's shop ran a little brook which was a never-failing delight. In the clam and muscle shells of its bed the cousins searched for pearls. Here, also, a dam was built, and soon a small saw-mill was in operation, which sawed miniature logs into very neat little slices. A quiet corner of the brook was arranged as an aquarium, and fishes were caught with a net in an adjoining pond and conveyed to their new home. Fishing with a hook was never an amusement for Frank. In fact, he would not take the life of even a mosquito. He was in great agony when he saw a mouse caught in a trap, and for several years was unwilling to eat meat, the thought of the death of animals caused him such pain. For that reason, he always spoke with horror of the profession of a naturalist. In later years, he was convinced that it was not always wrong to take life ; and, though he would not fish himself, he has been known to spend a morning, baiting a hook and removing from it the fish caught by a timid friend.

In 1859, with his father and mother, he made his first trip to the West. They visited Niagara Falls, Chicago, and St. Louis. A school composition written on his return, about the journey from Chicago to St. Louis, shows that he was keenly observant of the objects along the road. He speaks of the prairies, the railway tracks "straight as an arrow," the men he saw working bellows to supply air for the people in the coal mines, the "steamers and propellers plying in the dark muddy water of the

Mississippi," and the lager-beer shops and gardens of St. Louis. He was then twelve years old. Three years later, he went still farther west, extending his travels to Minnesota.

In 1860, after a long and painful illness, his beautiful mother died. She had been Frank's constant companion, and her loss caused him a deep and silent grief. After her death he remained for a time with an uncle, refusing to come home, as he could not bear to see the rooms where she had been.

The home still remained, though the mother was gone, for an aunt faithfully cared for the children.

Frank was so constantly poring over his books that his delicacy of appearance was more marked than ever. Wise people shook their heads and said he would never live to grow up. He once overheard such a remark, and, as he said afterwards, determined he *would* live. He no longer refused to eat meat ; later he went to the gymnasium, and by every sort of out-of-door exercise began to acquire the physical vigor which he exhibited in after years.

His visits to the woods of Maine assisted much in this development. In the summer of 1861, he first went with an uncle on an excursion into the wilds of Somerset County. They took long tramps through rough places, his companions stopping occasionally for trout-fishing ; but, as his uncle says, " it always hurt Frank's feelings to see the little trout taken out of the water to die" ; so they desisted from that sport after the first day. Once they surprised a fine covey of partridges. His uncle was preparing to take a shot ; but Frank said he would rather go without eating till he got home, than have one of the birds killed, so the indulgent uncle let them all fly away. Frank brought home sketches of the deserted logging-camps where they had passed their nights. The next winter he again slept in the same quarters, though this time there was no lack of company, for he found there twenty men, all strangers to him, engaged in hauling logs to be floated down Dead River. A few minutes after arriving, Frank was reading the war news to an eager crowd of listeners. His uncle says: " I never saw men in camp give such good attention to reading as they gave that night ; and when bed-time came, there was not a man in the crew but would have been glad to give up his berth to Frank." He visited the woods during the two succeeding winters, as well as in the intervening summers, sometimes climbing mountains so steep that it was necessary to draw one's self up by the bushes, and often sleeping in the open air on a fragrant bed of cedar-boughs. One of his Maine sketches is a view of Mount Katahdin, taken as he was crossing Moosehead Lake on a little steamer. He also took long rides about the country with his uncle, who was then deputy-sheriff, and whom he assisted in securing his prisoners and in making out his returns. His uncle speaks of the especial interest Frank had in talking with old people. He is still remembered by the family of a revolutionary soldier, with whom he once had a long conversation.

In Maine lived Frank's Grandmother Firth. She was a birthright member of the society of Friends ; but, marrying out of their society, had lost her membership in accordance with their rules, and she did not again unite with

them, although retaining their forms of speech, and their
hostility to human slavery and to war. She could relate
tales of events in English history, which happened near
the place of her birth, — Loughborough, in England.
Frank never tired of hearing of Richard III and Bosworth
Field ; and the old traditions, poems, and ballads which
she recited, had a strange interest for him.

Frank was never without some sort of pet. His earliest
ones had been some green snakes, which he taught to
twine themselves around his neck. When one of the
pets died, he used to make a coffin for it, and usually
performed some funeral service, while his sister and her
friends acted as mourners. He would afterwards place a
wooden slab to mark the place of interment.

By and by the father brought home a new wife who
became a mother to the children. She also was a Miss
Russell, though she came from Plymouth, Mass., and her
family were not related to the Russells of Charlton. Frank
loved and honored her as he had his own mother. She
thus writes of him : —

"Frank had early learned the lesson of obedience, a
lesson never forgotten, and accepted by him in its broad-
est sense, — obedience to authority and obedience to duty.
I have often thought of him, standing in the same stead-
fast spirit as Casabianca amidst the flames, if authority,
recognized by him as such, required it ; or walking firmly
to the cannon's mouth if duty led that way. What sac-
rifices of a strong, young will such an idea of obedience
required on his part, let any child of earnest purpose
answer.

"That which the boy asked of himself towards his

superiors in authority, the man had a right to ask from those in his service, and 'Mr. Firth' became a strict disciplinarian."

For a long time Frank had spent much of his leisure in observing the working of an engine used for sawing wood at the Boston & Worcester Railroad station. He now began to work with his jackknife on small wooden patterns, and one by one as they were finished he took them to the foundry. Finally, all the castings were brought home and fitted together, and the result was a horizontal stationary engine, of the following dimensions : length of stroke, $1\frac{3}{4}$ inches ; diameter of cylinder, $\frac{3}{4}$ inch ; length of main connection, 5 inches ; throw of eccentric, $\frac{3}{8}$ inches ; diameter of balance-wheel, 6 inches. The engine has four valves, two steam and two exhaust, each working independently. They are operated by two rocker shafts and arms, both being driven by one eccentric in a novel way, original with the builder, whose initials, F. R. F., are found on the casting which supports the main connection. Weight of engine, with black-walnut stand, 17 pounds.

Many evenings during the winter of 1863-4, by means of steam from a boiler (improvised from a soup-kettle), placed on the kitchen stove at home, the little engine worked to a charm.

In 1863, Frank graduated from the High School in Worcester, but remained there for another year, pursuing a few extra studies. To occupy his leisure he took to wood-engraving, copying many of the illustrations in Dickens' works. His blocks are really very nice specimens of carving. He also made various collections, which are still preserved, of coins, postage-stamps, autographs, and of curiosities in general. Several books he filled with the patriotic envelopes issued during the war.

He was naturally very sensitive, and shrank from all horrible sights. With the desire of self-conquest always evinced by him, he sought to overcome this feeling. He obtained bloody relics of battle-fields, visited the hospitals, and always tried to see the sufferers by street or railway accidents. Later in life, he came to regard this as a morbid practice, and avoided such sights.

In the spring of 1864, Frank had a desire to go to West Point, on account of the advantage there afforded for the study of engineering. A letter obtained to send with his application, written by Mr. Harris R. Greene, under whose instruction Frank had been for five years, characterized him a " young man of more than ordinary scholarship and of more than ordinary ability," and mentioned that his marks had ranged from 98 to 100 on a maximum of 100, and that he had taken two prizes in the school.

Frank did not obtain the appointment. At that time there were so many applications for the sons of soldiers, that the chance of others was small.

He had taken the so-called " classical course " at school, fitting him for college ; but, as a college education would not prepare him for his chosen career, it was thought best for him to wait a year before deciding where to continue his studies.

During a part of that year he worked as clerk in the Boston and Worcester freight office, at Worcester, thus gaining a practical insight into that department of a railway.

It was finally determined that he should go to the Institute of Technology, in Boston, then just starting upon its second year. In September, 1865, he entered, a year in advance, thus becoming a member of the pioneer class of the Institute. A month after, the family removed to Boston, Frank's father being called to the superintendency of the Boston & Worcester Railway. During the next three years, Frank was, as always, a careful student.

One of his classmates thus writes : —

" He was regarded as entirely unique among us. There was very little fellowship, though a great deal of good feeling between him and his companions. His habits of study were such as to prevent much familiar intercourse with others. Always book in hand, his studying was largely done in the odd moments between lectures and in the snatches of time to be caught during recitation. The games which most young men find necessary to keep alive their energies, he did not join in ; but he showed a desire to master their science and to learn about them by shorter methods than playing. His power of abstraction was so great that he mastered facts very readily, and in recitation he was very keen, and a sharp questioner."

He was not, however, so occupied with his studies as to be debarred from the newly-opened opportunities of a large city.

It can only have been by means of great industry and the economical use of every odd moment that he was able to devote so many evenings to amusement. Into concert-room and theatre he carried the same keen and alert spirit which marked his every-day life. Wit and humor were not kept waiting for his laughter, nor pathos for his quick emotion, strong though scarcely shown. His taste was delicately appreciative, rather than critical ; indeed, where he liked, he did not care to criticise, but would idealize, rather ; and it was ever the best and purest that met with his approval.

Miss Maggie Mitchell, with her interpretation of the pathetic, wayward child-woman, was one of his great favorites, and many a happy two hours has he spent, charmed by the simple witcheries of " Fanchon," of " Little Barefoot," or of some sister character.

He lost no opportunity of seeing Madame Ristori in her grand impersonations, and he was seldom absent when Madame Parepa-Rosa's voice could be heard ; indeed, he admired the latter on her first coming to Boston, before she gained the popularity she has since enjoyed.

One of his old friends, referring to opportunities of this sort, writes : —

" I think that until he had them, he always fought against recreation; but his Boston experience seemed fully to wake him up to the use of pleasure, though he never could be persuaded to let pleasure master him."

His visits to the Athenæum library, access to which had been kindly procured for him by a friend, were a source of great enjoyment. He also passed many hours at the Eliot-street gymnasium.

During all this time, he was faithful in his attendance at church, usually going with the family to the Rev. James Freeman Clarke's Chapel, but often walking to Roxbury to hear there the Rev. Dr. Putnam.

In 1863, he began the plan of summer excursions. With his friend, Ben Watson, as a companion, he left Plymouth in a lobster smack which was to find her market in New York City. She touched at the end of Cape Cod, where the boys landed, and the same night they entered Provincetown, the "City of Fish-Flakes," which last were a source of continual amusement to Frank. Thence they walked along the Cape to Plymouth, a distance of one hundred and twelve miles, completing the trip in five days. Mr. Watson says : —

"We found the people very kind, and always ready to take us in for meals or lodging, very often refusing to take any pay. The longest walk we took at once was between Yarmouth and Sandwich, — about twenty-nine miles."

The next summer, with a third companion, the two started in the same smack, this time completing the trip to New York City. The first day, Frank and one of the friends resolved to begin to acquire the tan they so much admired in sea-farers ; so they went to sleep on deck in the sun with their arms bared to the elbow. The burns thus caused were so severe that they did not wish to repeat the experiment.

From New York they took steamer to Newburg. July 11th, they bade good-by to the Hudson, and (with the exception of a few days passed at Mt. Washington, Mass.), were travelling till August 3d, when they reached the Connecticut River, at Springfield, and took the cars for home, having "walked some three hundred miles and consumed ninety-five quarts of milk." They had climbed Mount Greylock, visited the Hoosac Tunnel, and the Shaker Village.

Mr. Watson says : —

"During this time, we slept out-of-doors almost every night, and very rarely took a regular meal at a table, but

2

we lived in fine style on bread and milk, berries, smoked beef, maple sugar, and hard bread. The latter articles we would buy in some town and carry with us in our knapsacks. We were often taken for returned soldiers, and in the cities we had very advantageous offers to enlist."

From passing so many nights in barns they became familiar with the sounds of various domestic animals, and on their return were able to astonish their friends by frightfully good imitations of them.

In the summer of 1865, with his tried companion, Frank spent about ten days walking through the White Mountains. 1866 found the two friends visiting the Forks of the Kennebec. Later in the same summer, Frank started alone by steamer for the Provinces. " St. John's," he wrote, " seemed strange and foreign ; large ship-yards and great piles of lumber all around the deep, narrow, steep-walled harbor." Halifax he found a "real English provincial town, old family mansions, moss, and respectability, shaded walks, knockers, chimney-pots, curtained beds, carafes for water, barracks, sunset guns, gala dress, and soldiers' parade, — everything as un-American as Quebec." (He had visited Quebec the preceding spring.)

At Pictou he found "some little employment" for himself in the mines. This was a new experience which he highly enjoyed.

In the summer of 1867, he improved his last vacation by a more extended excursion. Saturday, May 18th, saw him the only passenger on the "Annie Royden," East-Indiaman, bound for Liverpool. His first letter written on board said : "It seems like a dream that I ever was anywhere but here. My trunk and dressing-case and cookies

argue that I 've friends somewhere on earth, or had before
I ceased to grow old ; for now we have no landmarks, —
it is only on the authority of the nautical almanac that I
have reason to believe the days are not identical."

He found a friend on board the ship, in the captain, who
was "twenty-seven, and a jolly sort of man when you get
acquainted," and with whom he spent many evenings at
euchre. He had taken guide-books, and meant to prepare
for the coming sights ; but he said, "Real application to
study is impossible. I would rather be a naturalist than
the captain of a sailing vessel. I should think monasteries
and nunneries could be best maintained on the water."

The events of the day were, breakfast at eight, dinner at
two, and tea at six. "The water is a mixture of Hooghly
and Cochituate," he said. "My lemons and maple sugar
quite prop me up."

As at Nova Scotia he was a miner, so here he became a
seaman, and kept his "log" for the friends at home. For
example : "Wednesday, 29th. Blowing hard from west.
Barometer slowly sinking since last night. Temperature,
50°. Stern windows closed to-day in anticipation of rough
weather. Barometer 28.95 in evening, lower than it has
been since captain left Calcutta. Expecting a gale, so
part of our sails are taken in. Sat in overcoat all day."

The gale came on, as the "log" for Thursday, 30th,
shows : —

"Began to blow early in the morning. Frequent rain
squalls. . . . About 7 P. M. a wave came over the side
and drenched several sailors. Pork and beef casks on deck
broke loose. We are followed, not met by the waves.
Log shows thirteen knots an hour."

His friends were not put off with this alone. "When you write me," he says, "don't tell how thermometer stands, or prospect of rain. You would n't be writing to me any more than I have been to you, so I 'll break in upon the log."

Now we get glimpses of himself: —

. "I have Boston time by my watch, and 't was like old times to go to bed at seven o'clock, as I did last night; but then, 't was ten here. . . . Never had any idea of how a great ship pitches and heaves, before. Fine time taking in the idea; got it well shaken down."

The gale blew them along so that June 6th they entered the Mersey, having had a passage of but nineteen days from pilot to pilot. "A steamer could n't have brought us from Newfoundland much sooner. 'T was a good passage and a pleasant one, and always to be remembered. . . . Within three or four miles of land, one feels the air almost close, hardly wishes to be nearer." He was not sorry, on the whole, to leave the sea, for he said : "Captain offers to take me to Calcutta and make a sea-captain of me, for forty pounds, — cheap, but no object. I don't want any more curry at present."

At the end of three days, which were spent in seeing the usual objects of interest about Liverpool, he went on to Manchester. Here he was naturally interested in the mills and machine-shops, several of which he examined, and next turned his steps toward Marsden, the little town where his father had gone to school as a boy.

Frank sought out the old schoolmaster, who was still living there, and wrote home about him as follows : —

"School was not keeping, but Joseph Webster sat at his

desk. . . . When I introduced myself, he said he remembered you well, and at once took from his closet his
accounts for 1826–7, and I saw how three quarters' school-
ing for Abraham and Samuel Firth had been properly paid
for, and when the books they used were each purchased.
The last receipt was August 20th, and 'gone to America'
closed the account."

After making excursions to Ripon, Fountain Abbey,
etc., he went on to York and saw the grand old minster.

At Leeds, he again inspected iron-works, and then continued his journey to Halifax, wishing to see this town,
because, as well as Marsden, it had been one of his father's
homes in the old days.

At Leicester, he was joined by his friend and classmate,
Mr. James Tolman, who continued with him during the
remainder of the journey.

After seeing Kenilworth and Warwick, they visited
Oxford, whose ever-potent charm was enhanced by the
kindness of a family of relatives whom Frank found there.

" June 24th," he wrote, " we came to London, and there
we were entirely at home. The names on the 'busses,
the streets and public buildings, were old friends. We
walked into the city from Euston Square station, past
Gray's and Lincoln's Inn, down Fleet Street, under Temple
Bar, into the Strand. The Lord Mayor did n't unlock the
gates for us, because they were open."

The next week was spent in the keenest enjoyment of
London and its sights. They visited the British Museum
three times, where Frank took special interest in the autographs and old books. Kensington Museum delighted
him ; " I 'd give the seven miles of paintings at Versailles,"

he said, "and throw in the palace itself, for that Kensington collection."

They presented letters of introduction to the superintendent of the Southeastern Railway, and went to see railway shops on the Surrey side of the river ; also, to Greenwich Observatory, and "stepped into East Longitude" there. They heard Spurgeon at the Tabernacle, John Stuart Mill at a reform meeting in St. James' Hall, and later, heard Simms Reeves sing the " Bay of Biscay."

July 2d, they left London, and after a pleasant excursion to the Isle of Wight, to visit some relatives of Mr. Tolman, they "celebrated the Fourth by stepping into Europe, and for torpedoes in the evening, heard the Paris cabmen snap their whips."

Frank's first letter from Paris, dated " Vanity Fair, July 5th," and signed, "Your happy, roving Frank," said, " This is a Paris Sunday. The people are out, shops all open until noon and since tea, and these few minutes I have been thinking of you, are my only religious service to-day. . . . We are up six flights in the Rue St. Honoré, in the strangest old building, a real puzzle of a place, very like a prison. We pay fifty cents a day for lodgings. We have found the cheap way of Paris. It all depends on where you get your food. . . . We go to a crêmerie. . . . At the Royal Mews, in London, we saw carriages like the pumpkin Cinderella went to the ball in ; but Napoleon's carriages we have seen to-day at Versailles are indeed ' some punkins.' They outshine Vic.'s drays altogether."

" I 've heard ' Romeo and Juliet,' as like ' Faust,' in music and incident, as two things, not the same, can be ;

also, have seen the famous 'Hernani,' and Molière's 'Misanthrope' at the 'Comédie.'"

Five days in Paris were filled with industrious sightseeing, there being more objects of interest than usual, on account of the Great Exposition; and then, with full appreciation of its beauty and its wonders, they bade goodby to the gay capital, and turned their faces mountainward.

The principal points of their Swiss tour were as follows : —

From Paris to Neuchâtel, Lausanne, Vevey, Chillon, down Lake Geneva to Geneva, to Cluse, thence on foot to Chamouni; up the Jardin and Flégère, over the Mauvais Pas and Col de Balme, afoot from Chamouni to Martigny, and up the Grand St. Bernard to the Hospice; back again to Martigny, and so over the Alps to Italy.

Every hour in Switzerland was filled with delight. The weather, also, was favorable. Frank wrote : "We have seen Mt. Blanc free from shadow of a cloud at all times of the day (and by moonlight), and from many points ; so we count ourselves fortunate. Good wishes have proved very potent."

The great wonder of the mountains and the little novelties of daily life were alike charming. On their way down into the valley from a mountain, one evening, they lay for a while at their ease upon a great rock, with a "stunning landscape" stretching miles before them, and "were served a supper of goats' milk by a couple of nutbrown maids." . . .

"I've just eaten a real Swiss dinner-supper," he wrote ; "boiled eggs, coffee, honey, bread and butter; isn't it nice, when each article is the best of its kind, and a tolerable landscape thrown in ?" Even the earth yielded them its sweetness. "As for new-mown hay, we have n't been out of the scent of it in Switzerland, except when the grass was snow," he said.

Amid so much that was new and lovely, the friends at home were warmly remembered. "Don't call it superstition," he wrote, "but it is a real pleasure to show Mt. Blanc and St. Bernard to the tintypes."

These happy days were also very active. Many a mile did the friends swing along together on foot, delighted sometimes to show a chance pedestrian that Americans knew how to walk. For example : "These Englishmen annoy us a little. We have to outwalk and outclimb them whenever it comes to a trial, as it often does. Coming down from the 'Jardin' the home-stretch was a little severe ; the Islanders did n't look happy when they came in just too late."

One of the pleasantest episodes was a night spent at the Hospice of St. Bernard, as "guests of the hospitable fathers," where, after having been thoroughly drenched by the storm which still howled without, they enjoyed the bright fire and excellent fare, and passed the evening in listening to song and story from travellers of different nations, gathered into that safe refuge.

The next morning they trudged down the mountain again towards Martigny. Thence Mr. Tolman went by diligence, and Frank on foot, to Brieg (twenty miles), along the Rhine valley. Over the Simplon Pass they both walked, with a boy guide, to Domo d'Ossola. Next day a private carriage took them to Baveno, on Lake Mag-

giore. " The clouds would n't let us see Monte Rosa, but
they could n't help our seeing most lovely gardens, hill-
sides, houses, etc. They must have been characteristic
Italian scenery, for everything was new to us." At Baveno they heard reports about the cholera, which caused
them to turn about, "letting one Italian day suffice."
They took steamer across the lake, and "saw where the
drop-scenes find their subjects, — mountains, ruins, islands,
haze, etc.; you know how drop-scenes look." They landed
at Locarno, and were conducted by officials and followed
by the town's-people to a smoking-room, where, one by
one, they were "marched through stifling sulphur fumes
around a chafing-dish, and then released." "Italy was
taken in the plunge-bath way. The trip, through, was
a good deal longer than its hours, and will be remembered
like the first circus."

They walked over the St. Gothard Pass, finding it the
"most bleak and desolate mountain pass" they had yet
seen. Mr. Tolman took diligence over the Furca Pass.
Frank, as usual, walked ; "saw all there was to see, and
had a slide down a snow-field on a stone for a sled."
They met at the Glacier of the Rhone, "the noblest, broad-
est, eternal ice-river" they had seen. After a night at the
Faulhorn with "weather all that could be desired," they
went on through the Grindelwald Valley, up the Wengern
Alp, seeing two avalanches on the Jungfrau during their
ascent. " I'm glad," Frank wrote, " we saw the lower Alps
first; for after these Bernese monsters, a half-dozen more
than twelve thousand feet high, and with such charming,
picturesque surroundings, I never could have enjoyed as I
did even Mt. Blanc and Mer de Glace." From the Wen-

gern Alp down to Lauterbrunnen ; " the Valley of L.,"
he said, " is, without exception, as seen from above, the
most lovely place I ever looked upon ; every element of a
perfect picture, all the effects of climate, light and shade,
cultivation and wilderness, the Staubbach hanging from
the top of the limiting precipice." Thence their route
included Interlaken, Berne, Zurich, and Munich.

Munich they found " more American-like than any
city yet seen." They especially enjoyed the picture gal-
leries, where they learned to " pick out the masters " ; the
churches, the bronze foundry, and the collection of sculp-
ture. Of the latter, Frank said, " The two pieces I cared
for were the Sleeping Satyr (Barberini Faun), and Silenus
holding the infant Bacchus ; these two it was worth going
some distance to see."

Several evenings were spent at the theatres ; and one
evening they sat in the Beer Hall, with their " pints " of
Bavarian beer before them, and listened to " Sounds from
Home " played by Gungl's orchestra.

In Germany their school study of languages proved
practically useful. Frank wrote : " I find I can work along
in German much more readily than I could at first in
French. We have not had the smallest difficulty in making ourselves understood, and we now and then talk with
Germans about the 'wunderschön' and 'hübsch' views !
They all know a little English, and we know more German."

After leaving Munich and touching at Heidelberg, the
two travellers sailed down the Rhine from Mayence to
Cologne, taking time, of course, to see the cathedral
there, and then continued their course, by river and by

rail, to Amsterdam. The following letter gives Frank's own account of their visit to Holland and Belgium : —

LONDON, August 18, 1867.

"*Dear Father and Mother:* It is so pleasant to date one's self 'London,' that I can't help enjoying that luxury just once more. . . . Last Sunday evening (Aug. 11), we walked about the canal streets of Amsterdam. Dwellings and warehouses are frequently the same building, and no distinction is made in the busy town between streets to live in and streets to trade in. We went through the Jews' quarter ; streets were narrow and close ; washing hung out on racks from upper windows, the passage below crowded with children. (Never saw so many in an Irish neighborhood of twice the size.) They were trading among themselves actively, in small fish (which they fried publicly and sold hot), small fruit, vegetables, and a sort of pancake. At the railway station many small 'Aarons' meet each train and insist upon seizing your baggage to carry it. Two followed us a quarter of a mile, talking and attempting to grab our bags ; my follower finally tried to spit upon me and then followed a little way behind, shouting ; but we did n't give in. The whole atmosphere of Amsterdam is that of Plymouth about the water-side, everything sluggish and sunshiny ; the fine old leaning houses all seemed sleepy. I shall remember it until I see you.

"Monday afternoon, passing by rail from Amsterdam to Rotterdam, the uniform scenery was made up of rich, flat farms. The fields were sometimes defined by lines of living trees. The roads which crossed the track gave us glimpses now and then of forest tunnels one or two miles long. The houses and gardens were made by people whose idea of comfort was pretty much our own. We did n't see one of the typical Dutchmen (as common as Jonathans). We crossed the bed of Haarlem Lake, and, much of the way, had the sea-view shut out by the dike. We spent two hours in Rotterdam. The town was full of people (Annual Fair lasting a week), and we saw an unexpected show of booths and strolling players. If there is a harmless popular amusement in England or Central Europe that we have not seen, then fetch it on. We went by steamer from Rotterdam among the islands in the Delta of the Rhine, a couple of hours, moonlight part of the way, and then by rail from Moerdijh to Antwerp.

" Next day we climbed the famous cathedral tower, saw the pictures in the museum, but enjoyed much more the Rubenses I had seen elsewhere. In the Low Countries the laboring people generally wear the heavy wooden shoes (sabots), and in the morning you meet many women carrying fresh milk in pails hung by a yoke. The drink is neither wine nor beer, but Schiedam schnapps, or, in English, gin. Spent the afternoon of Tuesday in Brussels, and early next morning walked over Waterloo. The ground is smooth and rolling, all rich and well cultivated. We went to the top of the Lion Hill, Belgian Memorial Earth Mound, then by lane through the fields to Hougomont, saw the broken walls, the well, and the whole situation. The forests in the neighborhood of Waterloo are darker and denser (without any underbrush whatever) than any I know in America. You can look into black darkness from the travelled road by daylight. (*Note.* — The

only mosquitos we have seen or heard in Europe, attacked
us at Mount St. Jean, where we slept in the house in
which Victor Hugo wrote his famous account of the battle
of Waterloo.) We spent the next day in Brussels, visited
the very fine cathedral, rich in painted windows and wood
carving. Saw, as we have frequently elsewhere, educated,
interesting people kneeling at the altar, bowing and crossing themselves ; where the organ is sounding, boys singing, and sunlight streaming down in many-colored rays,
while other parts of the great church are cold and tomb-
like, every one must feel a sort of present Heaven, where
angels sing, and, at the same time, a sense of darkness and
coldness, which, by contrast, made those we saw shudder
as they moved closer to the candles, pictures, and singers
about the altar. We have now seen half the famous great
churches of Europe. We cannot describe them one by
one, but we have a cathedral idea which only experience
like ours gives.

"LONDON, MONDAY MORNING
(Very early for London), 6.30 A. M.

"From Brussels we went by rail to Ghent. . . . In
these Low Country railway stations, the signs Way Out,
Parcels Office, Refreshment Room, Ticket Office, etc., are
in four languages, Dutch or Flemish, French, German, and
English. The people all speak a few English words, and
the Dutch signs are all ludicrously English. 'Huis te huir'
(House to hire or let), 'Stoomboot' (Steamboat). We tried
to buy some milk to drink, tried German, French, and
English, and found it was 'mellac' we wanted. Belgium
is the pleasantest quiet farming country we have seen, a
sort of farmer's paradise. We liked people and country

very much. From Ghent we went to Ostende, and at eleven
in the evening, by the light of the full moon, started for
London, closing the forty-four days of continental travel.
The whole continental tour will cost one hundred and
twenty dollars in gold, and is, I consider, cheap for the
money. Next morning by daylight we came up the
Thames. . . . I am really very much attached to London.
No other city has the real charm, while London has none
of the unsatisfying glare. Yesterday morning I found
Temple Church closed ; so went up to Mr. Martineau's
and heard Mr. —— of Falmouth. Mr. M. is in the
country. Jimmy and I then went down to Westminster
Abbey, re-read epitaphs, and fixed in our minds the im-
pressive whole. In the evening we packed and wrote
home, and this is the plan we have laid : We leave here
by the Great Northern, reaching Boston early in the evening ; leave there to-morrow morning and sleep at Newcastle.
Wednesday morning, go from Newcastle to Edinburgh,
reaching there 11 A. M., and Thursday we go to Glasgow.
Friday we sail, Saturday touch at port of Londonderry,
and with good luck, surprise you at breakfast five days
after you receive this.

" In Europe we could know nothing of American politics.
Since our return we see that affairs are quite interesting,
and not a little disturbed.

"Now good-by and love to all,   FRANK,

Late of Europe, going to emigrate if there's any chance
for a young man out in your woods."

The above plan was carried out with the exception of
an additional week in Scotland. While in Glasgow, they

went down the Clyde to one of the famous ship-yards.
On the same excursion they "saw where Highland Mary
died, and stood beside her grave." Loch Lomond, Loch
Katrine, the Trossachs glen (peopled by the shadowy per-
sonages of the Lady of the Lake), Stirling Castle, and
Bannockburn, received each a hasty visit, much enjoyed
in spite of the prevailing Scotch mist. "Of course we
did n't see the top of Ben Lomond," Frank wrote, "but
we did see the heath-covered hill-sides, the beautiful
islands of both lakes, and, in fact, a good deal of Highland scenery, — were almost saturated with it."

The friends took steamer at Glasgow for home, August
30th, quite ready to rest on their coming voyage. Frank
appreciated both the repose and the oatmeal which the
"Caledonia" afforded, and often spoke of the latter dainty
as the chief charm of his homeward passage. On the 15th
of September he arrived in Boston, and, fulfilling his
promise, surprised the family at breakfast.

From both letters and words, it was plain that he looked
upon this journey as part of his education, as well as a
great pleasure. At one time while abroad, having received
news of the consolidation of the Boston & Worcester and
Western Railways, which he supposed might displace his
father, he wrote thus : ".I shall fill myself with what I see,
for I can do more for the family by making the most of my
present opportunities than in any other way, now and here.
I shall have a good time, — if the past is a sample, — a
very good time."

Towards the end of the trip he said, "We have employed
ourselves mainly in seeing and learning ; have not gone in
the beaten tracks altogether, and look upon few of our
days as unprofitably spent."

Mr. Tolman writes of his companion : —

"His energy and perseverance were marked characteristics, and were shown in the diligence with which he
worked to gain admission to some of the manufactories,
and in the general planning of our time, which was so arranged as to fill every hour of the day with sight-seeing,
leaving scarcely the necessary time for sleep and correspondence. As he was called shy and reserved, I was
surprised to find that he easily made travelling acquaintance, and we obtained much addition to our pleasure
from this fact. . . . He was fully impressed with the
American idea ; he wanted to see everything done on a
grand scale, and rapidly. In Germany, there was a good
deal of grumbling because of the slow method adopted to
transport travellers. . . . Anything like a swindle upon
the travelling public made him very indignant, and he did
not submit very gracefully to extortion."

From boyhood he had had the idea that he should prefer England to America. In all school discussions he
was found on the English side. He wrote for the school
paper a " Defence of ye much-abused and unpopular Tories
in ye Revolution of ye British Colonies in ye Continent
of America." He was inclined to think that we ought
still to be under British rule ; and when the Prince of
Wales was in this country, looked upon him as his future
rightful sovereign. Now, though he still loved England,
it was no longer first in his affections. He wrote, "Next
to America, England is the country of all those I have
seen that I would prefer to live in, if *I were not a day-
laborer.*" The first air we heard him play, the day he
returned, was, " Home again, from a Foreign Shore ! "

Henceforth all other countries were "foreign shores," and, as he often said, he "would be no other than an American citizen."

On the first of October the Institute opened, and our traveller became a school-boy again. He held a high position in his class, as in previous years, with apparently little effort. In fact, his constant complaint during that year was, that he had "not enough to do." He was never idle, however, as was shown by the constantly changing relays of Athenæum books on the table at home. Sometimes he might be seen doing his problems in the calculus, between the acts of the play or opera. He enjoyed the society of a few friends, but was never found in general company.

On the 26th of May, 1868, he was twenty-one years old. On that day he procured some work from an engineer's office in the city, and made known his resolve henceforth to support himself, which resolve was faithfully kept. He already had a small capital to begin with, which he had gained in the following manner : A gentleman having some bonds of various Western and Southern railways, about whose value he was doubtful, and lacking time himself for such business, entrusted their collection to Frank, who immediately wrote to the different business managers, and received many letters with printed headings. This was his first essay in railway correspondence, as well as in financial affairs. It proved a success, the amount of his share was more than he expected, and he was unwilling to take the whole of it.

3

The period of his boyhood ends here. We have dwelt so long upon the incidents of that time, because it will give his friends pleasure to recall them, and because we think they furnish a key to his subsequent career.

The annual examination held June 1st formed the termination of his course of study, and he began to prepare to carry out his long-cherished plan of going to the West to seek his fortune. On the 15th of June he set out.

He made a little call on an old school-fellow at West Point, but resisted entreaties to stay for class-day, as his "plans were laid." On the way he "looked Buffalo over, spent a day at Niagara, lounging about Goat Island and the Three Sisters, reading ' Old Curiosity Shop,' and pounding fossils out of the rocks, seeing the preparations for the new suspension bridge, and examining the railroad bridge critically."

At Detroit he stopped to present his credentials to Mr. Joy, the " Railway King of the West." This is one of them : —

" MASS. INSTITUTE OF TECH'Y, June 2, 1868.

" The bearer of this, Mr. Frank R. Firth, of Boston, having completed the full course of studies in this Institute, has recently passed his graduating examination and will receive his diploma in civil engineering at the time appointed for conferring degrees next October.

"'The abilities, industry and attainments which have won for Mr. Firth a very eminent position in his class cannot fail to secure his success as a Civil Engineer, or in whatever department of applied science he may be employed.

" WILLIAM B. ROGERS,
" *Pres. Mass. Inst. Tech'y.*"

Mr. Firth also had letters of introduction from some of the Boston capitalists who are interested in Western railways.

After waiting for some time, he had an interview of a few minutes with Mr. Joy. That gentleman acted with his usual promptness. " You 're Mr. Firth ? " he asked. Then he looked through the letters, and said at once, " I will give you work in Kansas ; I shall be ready in a fortnight ; you shall begin as engineers usually begin."

From Chicago, Mr. Firth, as we must henceforth call him, wrote his friends of his success. " The trunk had better come out as soon as it pleases," he said ; " I don't know what special outfit I shall require ; boots (very long-legged) will make an engineer of me, I think, as effectually as my prospective C. E."

The wonders of Chicago, the Pullman cars, stock-yards, water-works, elevators, etc., absorbed him for the next few days. Mr. H. E. Sargent, who acted as his host in Chicago, wrote to Mr. Firth's father : —

" You ought to feel very proud of Frank. *I* certainly should, in introducing him to our people, and my interest in his future will be very great. I never saw a *young* man so generally posted on all useful topics and subjects." The interest which Mr. Sargent then expressed in Mr. Firth never failed through all his subsequent career, and whether in sickness or health, he had no truer or more affectionate friend to look to, nor could Mr. Sargent have done more for him had he been his own son.

Mr. Firth proposed next, while awaiting his orders, to "travel off somewhere and see something." Cincinnati, Louisville, and Mammoth Cave were chosen.

July 7th, he started, by order of Mr. Joy, to report to Mr. O. Chanute, then engineer of the Kansas City bridge as well as of the projected Fort Scott Railroad. By the way, he visited the Clinton, Rock Island, Burlington, and Quincy bridges. He made himself known to the several engineers, and "talked with them about the structures, . . . getting the value of some days of 'red book'."

I He was at this time collecting material for his thesis (for which he had chosen the subject of bridge construction), to be handed in at the Institute before getting his degree in October. A letter written to his sister on the journey is an excellent example of the mingled current of fun and seriousness which ran through all he wrote and said : —

"Inspecting bridges does not fully satisfy me. I am now building one of paper from Missouri to Massachusetts ; expect that it will be complete in four days, and possess peculiar advantages ; cost is six cents, and if it breaks down nobody is hurt. We must come to paper for bridges, sooner or later."

In the same letter he said: "You should n't laugh at English people for their mistakes about the East, — the common ideas of the Western towns are almost as false. Quincy, where I have been, goes far beyond Springfield in the freshness and attractiveness of the private residences. The dresses are all in the same style, the airs hummed are just the same, the political talk is naturally about the same persons, and the Chickering pianos have a familiar sound."

Arrived in Kansas City, after climbing the bluff to see the town, he found Mr. Chanute, who kindly asked him to his house, and promised to give him " every advantage for

trying every branch of the service, and having the necessary practice in each."

Mr. Chanute writes : —

" We were at that time just taking charge of the Kansas
and Neosho Valley Railroad (now Mo. R., Ft. Scott, and
Gulf R. R.), which had been begun by a local company,
and had some twenty-one miles graded, from Kansas City
to Olathe. I told him I intended to walk over this grading
the next day to examine its condition, and when I returned, we would organize a party and give him a place in it.
He said at once that he would like to accompany me over
the road, as he had had some practice afoot in Switzerland
the previous year ; and with some misgivings as to whether
he would hold out, I consented. I remember the next day
was one of the hottest of that year, and our walk lay up
the valley of a little stream, bounded by high hills, and
through weeds higher than our heads. Four of us left
Kansas City about 10 A. M., but only two, Mr. Firth and
myself, held out to Olathe, the others having been com-
pelled to obtain horses, and follow the highway."

They reached Olathe the next morning, and found there
the party who were making preliminary surveys, Mr.
Chapman being engineer in charge. Mr. Firth joined
them as assistant, his pay being two dollars per day, and
board.

A new life now began for him. He wrote from camp
near Spring Hill, July 19th : —

" We are camped on the prairie, close by roads where
overland trains for Indian Territory pass. The mail for
Fort Scott goes each way once a day, and now and then
we see a stray Indian on horseback, with colored ribbons

around his hat. Law forbids driving herds of Mexican or Texan cattle through this part of Kansas, on account of a hoof disease they give the domestic ones; so they are driven through the western part, and shipped by rail. Our road is to bring them all by and by. The corps contains twelve men, one boy, two horses, one pony, and more men are coming. We live in three tents, besides the kitchen, and have a great, springless wagon to jolt to and from work in, and move the city from point to point. The officers are chief engineer, three assistant engineers, three non-professional assistant engineers, three axemen, one cook, one teamster, and one boy. . . . Rice, one of the civil assistants, is my special friend. . . . There are a great many snakes here, — no mosquitos. . . . We suffer more for want of water than for anything else. . . . I have fresh milk morning and evening, from a house close by, and have just got well into this manner of life."

The only other wants he mentions are "letters from home, and reading matter." "After a day's work," he said, "we are completely fagged out, have to lie down flat, and can read newspapers or novels with a relish, while we cannot study." A "Globe" edition of Shakespeare was sent him at that time. It went with him through all his after experience, and he even had it on the train at the time of the accident which caused his death. His family have it now, well worn and stained, but very precious.

He was quite annoyed by the visits of the men to a store in the village, where "an old joker sells lemonade, and they buy whiskey," the liquor law being then in force.

Mr. F. G. Rice, mentioned above, writes : —

" I remember as plainly as yesterday when Mr. Firth
came into camp. We had quite an argument whether he
was an Englishman or a Frenchman. We were sleeping
in what are called wall tents, six in a tent. As I was a
stranger in the party, the same as Mr. Firth, we slept together, he using the little knapsack he had on his travels
in Europe, for a pillow. He was my companion all the
time he was in the party. After he went in the other
party, he used to come over quite often and stay all night
with me. Every evening, regularly, he would take his
knapsack and go to a stream for a bath, if it was not
stormy. . . . The first day he was out in the party
he was back-flagman ; that is the easiest position in engineering, and is usually filled by a boy. When we came
in at night, I heard the engineer in charge say he was the
best back-flagman he ever had, that he was always ready,
and seemed to understand his business. The next day
he acted as topographer, which position he occupied until
he went into another party as rodman. . . . When he
first joined the party, he seemed afraid that the work
would not last long enough ; he would ask the engineer
what he should do the next day. I have spent a great
many pleasant hours reading papers and magazines which
he was kind enough to loan me. I don't think he ever
went out on the line without having a number of papers
in his pockets. If we stopped for five minutes, he would
commence reading ; and when they were ready to pro-
ceed, he would be one of the first to be ready. . . . I
never knew him to find fault but once, and that was one
day when we first started out. It was very warm indeed,
and water was very scarce. We did not get our dinner

till nearly three o'clock, and then it consisted of chicken soup and bread, and only half enough of that. For the first week or two, I thought he would not be able to stand it ; but he told me he was going to rough it through, and some day he intended to be superintendent of a railroad."

Mr. Chanute says of Mr. Firth at this time: "I know that he was always exceedingly willing and eager to learn, and frequently did more than was required of him."

The next Sunday letter, written from the same camp, is "founded on fact," and is full of detailed description of the new country : its townships, six miles square ; its one-hundred-and-sixty-acre farms ; its eighty-acre corn-fields, with corn ten feet in height ; its wonderful meals for "two bits (twenty-five cents)," and its "famous melon-patches." He enclosed some leaves of a plant called "rosin weed, or north and south plant," of which he said: "The independent fronds are almost exactly in the meridian, giving you north and south at once (not which is which, of course)."

July 30th, Mr. Firth was ordered to join a party who passed his camp on the way to survey the line south from Paola. He now served as rodman, Capt. Cozzens being in command. The company, with three exceptions, was made up of ex-rebels. One of the "exceptions" was Mr. Morison, of Massachusetts, who was temporarily acting as leveller.

The change was a welcome one for Mr. Firth. He wrote : " Here I have definite work which I have not had before. I am at the very bottom of the ladder ; my work consists in holding a rod up, and moving a target up or down as the leveller signals. It seems like punching a ticket as preparation for the railway service, but Mr. Chanute values the discipline, and I'm not going to object. . . . I carry a straight rod twelve feet long, a hatchet, and in the slack of my shirt a supply of wooden pins, a note-book in my overalls pocket, and I have a pencil tied to my button-hole. You can imagine how I look, with red shirt, blue overalls, and that equipment. . . . They talk of peach pudding and chicken for our three o'clock Sunday dinner. . . . South of Paola the country is much poorer than north of it."

The country, in fact, was full of miasma, and the two unhealthiest months were approaching. The next letter said, " I have been really sick."

The Twin Springs doctor prescribed for him, the camp was moved to a more healthy situation, with "plenty of cold, clear water," and in a few days he was on duty again. Camp-life with his present party seems to have been a novel experience. " I serve," he said, " to illustrate the fraternal feeling that can prevail between North and South. . . . The personal histories of our men, which I am learning, are interesting enough. . . . The captain is very kind to me, does everything in his power for me, offers everything he has to me, and says an encouraging word now and then. . . . We have a flute and excellent singers in the company, and these moonlight nights it is delightful to hear the old negro melodies, as the men lie around in the easiest of positions ; a better chorus of male voices I don't care to hear. . . . But for the drinking, our party would be entirely agreeable."

August 16th, by permission of Mr. Chanute, Mr. Firth left the camp, and after staying a night with his "first

party," went with Mr. Chap..nan to Kansas City. The
next fortnight he passed in that place, writing the thesis
on "Bridge Construction." It was "a digest of notes and
observations, to the tune of fifty pages," and was highly
commended by the professor to whom it was sent.

During this time he was the guest of Mr. Chanute,
thereby strengthening a very pleasant acquaintance.
After his out-of-door life of the last two months, a "pleasant and well-ordered" home was very delightful to him.
Much as he enjoyed camp, he had felt the want there, for
he said of it: "There's no such thing as time of your
own, no evenings, no Sundays, no retirement at all. The
experience in method, carefulness, responsibility, and
associations with all kinds of American types, makes a
year in the field a season well spent."

The "season" was not yet over. August 30th found
him in "Old Barracks, Paola," with Mr. Chapman's party.
They were ordered back to Spring Hill, from which
point they were to "mark out work for the contractors,
and work their way south again." Mr. Firth remained
with them, acting as leveller, until September 13th, when
he rejoined his "own" party (under Capt. Cozzens), four
miles below Ossawatomie.

Speaking of a visit to that town, he said: "I wanted to
send you some relic of John Brown's house; but he did n't
live in Ossawatomie, but twelve miles west."

He still performed the duties of leveller (with the exception of a few days when he was rodman), though it was not
till early in October that he received his appointment to that
position, with one hundred dollars a month, and board. He
wrote September 15th: "My rodman and I have done a good

day's work, levelled three and a quarter miles and drawn
profiles of the work. My rodman is Lon Wiggin, one of the
best singers in camp, besides being a much better rodman
than I was, I think. . . . If the road should follow the route
we have surveyed, the traveller will get as false an idea of
Kansas as the mere river traveller does of the Mississippi-
divided States."

He elsewhere said : " This district is peopled by natural
paupers ; no chickens, no eggs, no butter, no beef, no sweet
potatoes, and nothing but their laziness and lack of capital,
which is the result of previous laziness, to thank for it.
They will not drive less than two horses, and will not walk
to a place they wish to reach, but rather walk the same
distance to hire a team to carry them to the first point."

These people were generous, by his own showing.
" Peaches are very plenty here, twenty-five cents a bushel,
and free to railway men. While the party camped near
Mound City, a great dish of peeled and cut peaches was
sent to camp every evening, with two or three quarts of
the richest cream ; and the whole 'outfit' was invited to a
grand supper before they came away."

September 17th, the first frost came. On the 18th,
Capt. Cozzens was superseded by Capt. Runk, of whom
Mr. Firth wrote : " He says little, but makes his work
out and means to have it done, and that without delay."
As to the direction of their survey, he said : " Between the
valleys of the Neosho and Marmatan there is a great, unsettled band of reserved land ; our line is down this ' divide,'
the water-shed between the Missouri and Arkansas Rivers."

After a certain amount of field work, the party would
camp at some convenient point, in order to finish maps

and profiles, and copy note-books to be sent to head-quarters; and, this accomplished, they would move on again. A letter written in October, said: "For six weeks I have not slept twice in the same township. It somehow piles up weeks of experience, this settling down and living, though only for twelve hours, in some place all new and not to be visited again."

Even the common Western expressions had their interest for him. "—— is preparing his 'outfit,'" he wrote. "He uses the word in ten thousand senses. Every instrument or article is an 'outfit' to him. He will wind up his 'outfit,' spread out his 'outfit,' have an early breakfast for the 'outfit;' and if he sees a strange object, asks, 'What outfit's that?'"

Many a long, active day was spent on the prairie, ended perhaps by a walk across country, by shaded cañons, and through a brook or two, to the camp which had moved during the day; finding it by "a sort of sense of locality, a geographical instinct that grows in one unconsciously, so that without any of the conventional landmarks, roads, houses, spires, etc., people can make and keep appointments in the wilderness, . . . defining localities particularly by their drainage."

At leisure moments Mr. Firth always turned with eagerness to his reading, finding interest in subjects the most diverse. He wrote, "I've read King John, the last 'Littell' I received (every article), and am now reading 'Jane Eyre,' and Isaiah." In such hours as these Kansas vanished "like the smoke its name signifies." All the letters received at home during this period were written in good, even high spirits, and were full of the new, free life. He

was learning, also, to take care of himself. He said : " I 'm
a notably prudent old boy now. Sometimes I assume a
character, advise myself, and laugh myself into real
common-sense, precaution, and care."

Early in November, though the beautiful Indian-sum-
mer days still lingered, the party began to find it necessary
to prepare for winter, and the hazy evenings out-of-doors,
lit by the dull glow of distant prairie fires, were soon ex-
changed for hours beside the comfortable stove, and can-
dle-light within the canvass walls. By the middle of the
month the creeks were up, delaying the mails, and winter
stood close at hand. " The early evening is a noisy time
here," he wrote, "all hands cutting or bringing wood for
the fires. Last thing before we lie down we fill our stove,
open the door, and the firelight fades into dreams."

November 29th, Mr. Firth wrote from camp, near Twin
Springs : " The weather ' beats me ' : lovely and vile.
When you 've lost all patience with rain and darkness and
mud, summer comes again, and next day the water at
the door is solid, and your coffee-cup is your finger-warmer.
. . . Why was n't Egypt plagued with mud ? Pharaoh
would have needed extra hardening to have held out then,
if business had called him through the corn-fields." And
again, December 6th : " Eight inches of snow upon the
ground, and the wind roaring through the great oaks."

In December it became so very cold, the snow lying
thick on the ground, that the most courageous of the
party could not but be glad that work in the field was
almost ended. They looked back with satisfaction on the
fact that they had " run one hundred and seventy-five
miles in two and a half weeks, much of it through timber,
and across a number of creeks."

For some time Mr. Firth's letters had often spoken of his coming visit home, disguising in fun of all sorts his strong desire to see his old friends once more. " Look out for the comet about to enter your system," he said. " Father sent me postage-stamps enough to come by mail ; but as there may be delays, I prefer the ordinary channels."

He reached home about the 20th of December, and remained a fortnight. Every hour of his stay was filled. There were all the friends to see in Charlton, Rochdale, Plymouth, and Boston, and the theatre was doubly attractive from his long abstinence. The time glided away so rapidly that his friends could scarcely realize he had been at home, except by looking at the Christmas presents he had taken so much pleasure in buying with his own earnings.

In earlier days, while dependent on his father, Mr. Firth had chosen to live with Spartan frugality, spending only what was absolutely necessary, though no restriction was ever placed upon him in that respect ; but once fairly in possession of an income, his generous gifts kept pace with his growing resources, and no pleasure was greater to him than the ability of thus giving expression to his warm feelings ; nor did he, later, deny himself those nice or beautiful articles for which he had always had a taste.

The vacation ended, he travelled westward for the second time. The rails on his own road were then laid only to Olathe, and on reaching that point, January 8th, he started to walk to Paola. "I packed my knapsack," he wrote, "slung my leather boots over my arm, and knee-deep in my 'gums,' struck out for a bourne from which no traveller had returned for some days."

Apropos of the muddy roads, over which it had taken the stage from Fort Scott three days and three nights to make a journey of eighty miles, Mr. Firth wrote: "Travelling in the last century in the interior of England no longer puzzles one who has seen the price every rich farming district must pay for its soil."

From Paola he set out to find Capt. Runk's camp, "following the stakes of his line over the prairie."

He was soon settled once more in the now familiar tent life, working as hard as the weather permitted, though not so steadily as he would have liked. "The truth of it is," he said, "we're having a very dull time, hampered by storms and rising water."

A letter written at this time shows that then, as always, he felt keenly the suffering of animals. He said: "We see cattle here starved for economy's sake, and fodder rotting in the corn-fields, kept for a higher price. . . . The worst feature of all their shirking, thriftless mismanagement is their abuse of cattle. I say what I think as often as I have opportunity, and they allow that it is all true, but say they have n't any capital, which is anything but a justification."

It troubled Mr. Firth that he could not get on with his work fast enough. He had sometimes to wait for those ahead of him in the field; and of one such occasion of enforced leisure he wrote: "I have been reading Scott, lying in the tall grass, . . . an anecdote of real border warfare now and then keeping one clear of Sir Walter's magic transformation of old-time border ruffians."

His literary pleasures were shared with those about him. Speaking of his companions, he said: "I keep them read-

ing during the long evenings, and generally find something to suit all tastes; 'Kenilworth,' 'Mary Barton,'
'Foul Play,' and 'Woman's Kingdom,' have been read
by all."

It was in these days that he obtained, in the absence
of the camp-cook, his first experience in the culinary
art, and made, according to his own testimony, excellent
"johnny-cake."

For some time he had been feeling that, while he loved
its "wandering freedom," he had learned whatever his
present life could teach. In fact, he was quite discon-
tented, and could be cheerful only by an effort. "I walked
myself into good humor and courage," he said. Having
written about the state of things to his father and Mr.
Sargent, he received letters advising his return home. He
by no means considered that his time had been lost, however. "If I do not learn to do many things here," he said,
"I do learn to be careful. I am laughed at a little for taking so many precautions." And again : "I checked levels
yesterday, and found that the difference between two independent lines of above seven miles each, was eleven
hundredths of a foot, or one inch and three tenths for fifteen miles of work ; so I am satisfied that I have mastered
the practical part of levelling." When away from camp
for a few days, the leveller who took his place found, on
comparing Mr. Firth's record with that of an intersecting
line, that the two differed by nine feet ; but on further examination, Mr. Firth's was found quite correct. He said
himself, that in one hundred and fifty miles of work, he
never had to go back a foot because of mistakes.

Towards the latter part of February, 1869, he wrote to

Mr. Chanute, asking to be transferred to a party on construction, and added, "I trust I do not make personal advantage my chief aim; at any rate, I try to be faithful and energetic in all company matters."

A favorable answer was soon received, for on March 15th he wrote: —

"In my pocket is an order to report to the captain who has charge of the construction of section four of the road. I join him as first assistant, and regard the change as in fact promotion. . . . My whole connection with this company of men has been pleasant; we have roasted, thirsted, frozen, and feasted together, travelled several hundreds of miles upon our work, and camped in company in some forty places. I shall always remember them, and the very pleasant scenes and times we have enjoyed; but I am glad to break my shell, and expand into new surroundings and more responsibility."

Mr. Chanute thus speaks of the division (No. IV) to which he was ordered: "This was the most difficult and interesting division on the road, having a greater variety of work, and requiring greater attention than any other, and it was for that reason that he was assigned to it."

Captain Runk, whose company Mr. Firth was leaving, afterwards wrote to him as follows: "During all my experience in my profession, I never have been attached to or had charge of a party where I found a person comprehending and executing his duties with more efficiency, promptness, and ability, than yourself. The fulness of your notes is good testimony as to your efficiency with the transit, and the record of your levels is as complete as any I ever saw rendered."

4

On the 15th of March, Mr. Firth, finding no conveyance at hand, "fell back on natural resources," and walked
thirty miles to " Hell's Bend," to join his new party, where
he found one hundred and twenty men shovelling and
wheeling, and work in full activity. He acted as first assistant, under Capt. Kirkpatrick, his pay being the same
as before, $100 a month.

The party was stationed not far from Twin Springs, and
Mr. Firth occupied, with the captain, " such a cozy shanty,
24 by 12, with real doors and windows." He wrote, April
4th : —

" We have two rooms, office and quarters, light, clean,
warm, and, best of all, roomy, with chairs to sit on, and a
table to write upon, which I have so much missed. A
neighbor furnishes meals for ten men and myself, at two
bits apiece."

The captain proved a congenial companion. Mr. Firth
wrote : —

" It is pleasant to pass my evenings with him, and I
count myself fortunate."

The work seems to have been no less to his taste.
" Captain gave me three miles at end of the division, and
told me not to come back till I had done everything
that was necessary ; that's experience of the right
sort."

March 27th, he said : " I have now to do directly with
many men ; and encourage them, while walking or resting, to tell me what they've been doing since they did
anything."

At this time he constantly spoke of disorderly proceed-
ings in the neighborhood, though he also said, " I 've never

had an uncivil word from a man." "Any one of the large
cities is far more unsafe than this country."

As spring advanced, his out-of-door life became more
and more pleasant, and he expressed, sometimes quaintly
enough, his enjoyment of nature. "To-day (March 28)
. . . the buds are budding and the bees beeswaxing," he
said. . . . "Birds are very plenty here, meadow-larks,
singing quails, whistling redbirds saying, 'pretty, pretty,
pretty,' bob-whites declaring their name, and a great many
unintelligible chatterers, besides booming turtle-doves."

Mr. Firth's ultimate aim was to be a practical railway
man, and his plan was to learn all about a railroad from its
beginning. Thinking he had had enough of this preliminary experience, and considering, also, the mental and
social advantages of which he had so long been deprived,
he seriously thought at this time of returning to the
East.

March 28th, he wrote : —

"In six weeks we shall have the work all laid out, and
a large part of it executed. The experience will then be
complete. I shall have taken part in railway construction
from the beginning to the end, the proper first experience
of a railway man."

A visit from Mr. Chanute in May, however, "put several
things in a new light." Mr. Chanute writes : —

"I went down to see him, and told him it would be much
better and safer for him to make haste slowly, and remain
with us ; as although he had ability to take a higher
position, he yet lacked experience of work and men, and
might fail if surrounded with less friendly influences. He
at once consented to remain, and has since repeatedly

thanked me for preventing what his maturer judgment taught him would have been a mistake."

Mr. Firth decided to stay at least until August, and wrote of the work : " Building the road becomes interesting and exciting. . . . Those dear old rails are coming nearer and nearer."

May 26th, he said : " My best birthday present is promotion. A division in Cherokee Lands is placed at my disposal." And again : " My experience on this division has been very pleasant indeed. I came here not knowing a single soul, and now I am on speaking terms with one hundred particularly, and four hundred more. I almost forget that my name is Frank."

He was not to leave his friends, however. The hostile settlers on the Cherokee Reservation prevented the road from being constructed at that time, and on the 23d of June, he became division engineer in place of Capt. Kirkpatrick. He really had performed the duties for some time, as the captain had been much with his family, who were living some few miles away.

It was eleven months since he began at the bottom of the ladder in field practice, and he now had but two superiors on the road, — Col. Smith, the Resident Engineer, and Mr. Chanute, the Chief.

He wrote : " What I always wanted was oportunity, and now I have it." . . . " It seems very odd to me when I say that a great railway bank must be made fuller on a given side, a ditch cut at a certain point, masonry pulled down and rebuilt, rocks blasted out of the way, trees cut down, great rock-cuts made deeper or wider, etc. ; that all these things should be done without ques-

tion, and that I should be appealed to to settle matters
in dispute between laborers. But I do like to parade up
the line in my broad-brimmed hat, with flowing blue
overalls tucked into my boots, and an unexceptionable
linen coat, followed by my 'subs,' carrying instruments,
measuring-rods, and axes. It will be the ruin of me."

His friends had no such fear, for the same letter said,
" No titles, please ; F. R. Firth, Twin Springs, Linn Co.,
Kansas, is sufficient to find me." Such was always his
feeling. At another time he said : " If you please, I would
rather not be addressed as Mr. ; simply, F. R. Firth. My
grandma left me the Quaker instinct, and to my feeling
rings and studs, hair-oil and complimentary titles, are
distasteful."

His pay was now advanced to $150 a month, without
subsistence. He had been sending checks to his father
for investment, from time to time. As his capital was increasing, he began to have an eye on the money market,
remarks in his letters showing that he kept track of the
fluctuating values of stocks. Alluding to his accumula-
tions, he wrote : " If I could economize like Thoreau, I
might begin the life and study of philosophy, for nine
cents a day is secured."

June 12th, he said : " Within the past week two shanties
have been built close by, and a village is really growing
up where we opened the ball." The place is now called
Les Cygnes. He said of it : " This is an unhealthy
district ; but knowing that, I take special precautions.
1st. Am not out-of-doors after sunset ; 2d. Breakfast first
thing in the morning ; 3d. Never miss a regular meal ;

4th. Eat nothing which is at all unphysiological. The result has been perfect health and sounder sleep than usual for the last month."

He had need to keep his health, for three months of very hard work followed. There was "a river to cross three times, a lake, a broad marsh, half a dozen hills to cut through, and very little prairie work."

Mr. Rice says : " I was with him nearly two months at Les Cygnes. Although I had to work hard, I had a very pleasant time while I was there. . . . He used to be bothered a great deal, nights, by bugs getting into the ink. He would have a saucer of water on the table, and when one would get into the ink, he would take it out carefully, and, after washing it, let it go. There were some bugs that I think visited the office every night. Mr. Firth would have a particular name for each one, and talk to them the same as if they were human.

" He was very careful not to expose his men too much. Every morning a heavy fog would rise from swamps in the neighborhood. He would keep the men in the office until the sun was high enough to drive it away. He was very careful of his own health, and seemed to be afraid that he would be taken sick and could not finish the work."

He determined to make his the " star division," and his whole heart was in his work. His letters became shorter now, and were all on one subject. One of them said : " At one point we now have carpenters, graders, and pile-drivers, working close together ; blows of the hammer, cutting of timber, blasting of rocks, making a pleasant chorus, for me at least. . . . Mr. Aiken and I walked a

mile by moonlight to admire a ditch finished that afternoon, and listen to the running water."

Mr. Firth was constantly going about with his friend,
Mr. Aiken, the superintendent of contractors, from whom
he said he received "many useful hints," the two only
disagreeing about the merits of their respective horses.

Mr. Firth's pony (Kit) was a great pet, and annual
contributions were sent in her name to the Massachusetts
Society for the Prevention of Cruelty to Animals.

Mr. Chanute writes, that during this time Mr. Firth's
" work was so well done, and the accounts he gave of it
so clear and precise, that Mr. Smith repeatedly called my
attention to it."

Speaking of a visit from Mr. Chanute and Mr. Smith,
Mr. Firth said : "All their criticism was praise." And
again : " Mr. Smith is my tower of strength ; whatever I
do, he sustains me in it."

Damages caused by a freshet helped to make the days
busier. July 25th, Mr. Firth wrote : " Saturday keeps
coming round, always welcome but hardly ever expected."

Outside interests were not quite forgotten, however.
" What is the general feeling in regard to the Alabama
Claims ? " he wrote. " Are we all ready for a war ? If it
comes, I am ready." At the same time he said : " I watch
for that locomotive. . . . Seven months deprived of
sounds I like so well, have made me hungry for bells and
whistles and rumbling wheels."

The division was at length finished. Mr. Firth wrote,
September 29th : " The track is laid to the end of my
fifteen miles, and in a couple of days I shall finish my
accounts. It does not seem right to me that trains should

be coming and going, men working and business being carried on here, in which I have no concern ; so a hen feels when her ducks take to water. Reason concedes that it is proper that a railway shall be used after it is built ; for all that, I feel like ordering the intruders off. My time has certainly come."

The last month had been very unhealthy, so that at one time Mr. Firth had written : " I should have to think awhile to recall five men of all I know who are not injured in health." On leaving, he said : " It will certainly be pleasant to cease to be a prisoner after dark, and to see the faces of healthy people about me " ; and it was joyfully that he wrote in his last letter from Les Cygnes : " Boston via Chicago will be the label for my button-hole."

He now proposed, after having seen how roads were surveyed, located, and built, to learn how they were operated ; so he bade good-by to Kansas, with some regret, after all ; for " the disagreeable things," he said, " have been trivial, and good health, active service, and my little household have given me unceasing pleasure."

The following note, received after reaching Boston, explains itself : —

"KANSAS CITY, Oct. 15, 1869.

" F. R. FIRTH, Esq.

My Dear Sir: . . . . I cannot allow our connection to close without expressing to you how perfectly satisfactory your attention to the work has been, and complimenting you upon the skill with which your division was finished. Beginning a perfect novice with us a little over a year ago, we have all been quite pleased with your rapid progress, and are sorry that your future plans do not lead you to remain with us.

Accept, however, my best wishes for your future prosperity, and believe me

Respectfully,

O. CHANUTE,
Chief Engineer."

The autumn was occupied in "inspection of and by relations," as Mr. Firth called it, and in visits among his many friends. His accounts of life in the field were ever new to them. They all felt that a man had come back in place of the boy, they had parted with so little while before.

Winter came, and brought the many attractions of theatre, concert, and opera, all keenly appreciated. He had the opportunity of seeing "Hamlet" played by Mr. Fechter (then almost unknown in Boston), whose entirely novel rendering of the character surprised and delighted him. "I, too, never realized the human interest of which the play is so full, before," he wrote to a friend.

At this time Mr. Firth took a course in bookkeeping at a commercial college, hoping to improve his hand-writing. Some people, it is true, have since doubted his success ; but he certainly tried.

He also became a visitor for the Boston Provident Association, his duty being to visit the poor of a certain district (Oneida Street, we believe) and ascertain their needs, drawing from the treasury of the association for their relief. The secretary of the society considered Mr. Firth one of the most judicious visitors he had known. Towards the really deserving he was liberal ; but he was quick at detecting impostors, and such had no countenance from him.

One old woman we know still remembers him as her
" darlin' visitor."

He assisted his father at the railway office a part of each
day, and spent many hours at the Athenæum, as here-
tofore. He was more in the society of friends than
formerly, his Western life having removed some of that
shyness which had before deterred him from it.

Notwithstanding all this employment, he was restless,
— longing for steady occupation. As no opportunity for
a satisfactory position on an Eastern railway offered, his
thoughts were tending westward. A letter to Mr. Chanute,
written in December, brought a reply promising him the
building of a division on the new Leavenworth, Lawrence
and Galveston road, and requesting him to report at Lawrence, on the first of March, 1870.

Now, for the third time, he left Boston, and though he
still desired to, and did, pay his taxes there, henceforth
his true home was to be Kansas.

On arriving at Lawrence, he was assigned, as his first
duty, the examination of the Kansas River for a railway
bridge (since built substantially on the line which he
located), — " a work much to my mind," he said. Mr.
Chanute writes : —

" He then began making a set of land record maps of
our line, so that he might have some practice in learning
the best way of preserving a record of the right of way,
land titles, etc., of a new railway. This information he
subsequently put to good use on the A. & N. R. R., where
such matters were found to be in considerable confusion."

This work occupied him for the next fortnight, which
time he passed in Lawrence, making the Leavenworth,

Lawrence and Galveston office his head-quarters, and
spending a "couple of hours" every evening at the
public reading-room.

There were two other Boston boys in the office, both of
whom accompanied Mr. Firth, when, about the middle of
March, he went to Iola to take charge of his division (No.
IV), which was twelve miles long. He was glad to find
his old friend, Mr. Aiken, at work there, as well as his
"faithful Hector," who had been with him at Les Cynges.

The brick house occupied by the railway offices served
as lodgings for Mr. Firth and his assistants. He took
great pride in his "family," which he said was "very har-
monious." The droll stories that were brought together
from the varied experiences of its members, gave him much
hearty enjoyment. He sometimes, however, passed pleasant evenings by himself. For instance : " To-morrow," he
wrote, " the party go to the south, and I shall have ghostly
company from the dear old books."

He threw himself just as earnestly into his work here as
he had done when on the Fort Scott Railway. April
24th, he wrote : —

"There is twenty times the satisfaction in every day
of these duties, than in such weeks as I spent in Boston ;
mind, I don't say enjoyment, but honest, hearty satisfaction, entirely without anxiety or hurry. I am not such a
nervous, uneven-tempered, angular piece as you knew me
at home."

Here is a sample of one of his satisfactory days, April
26th : " I rode, after breakfast, five miles to Deer Creek,
where there is a large party digging out bridge foundations. I gave them further instructions, centred the daps

(you won't find this in any dictionary), examined earth-
work and accepted several hundred feet of finished grading ; then returned to town in forty minutes, and dined.
After dinner, examined other work near town ; then sent
one of my boys, with instruments, five miles south of here
to work, and remain over night, and the two others I
directed to set finishing stakes upon a quarter of a mile of
work, two miles from town. I worked upon estimates in
the office until four, slept from four till five, and then walked
down the line, to see if the trees at Elm Creek had been
chopped down as I ordered them to be this morning, and
that the first grading force south of town was working
properly. The air was cool and fresh, and I was at my
boarding-house at six, where I read ' Littell ' by an open
window, until half-past, when my two favorite sons arrived,
and we eat. Since tea I have worked two hours on estimates."

There were some hours of recreation, however ; for he
mentioned, one evening in April, going to see " Fanchon "
performed in an unfinished store by a " Mammoth Combi-
nation Theatre Company, from New York."

He said in a letter to a friend : " You ask that I should
write what I am thinking of. Most of my waking thoughts,
and unfortunately sleeping thoughts too, occasionally, are
about how much bracing will be necessary for an abutment;
shall I oblige a man to haul material eight hundred feet
or allow him to cart it away, and replace in the bank at his
own expense ? How much of a gratuity shall I allow the
men who found clay instead of earth to build their bank
from ? how shall I arrange that work may be done in three
places to most advantage ? etc. I have enough to think

of, and questions of a sort that have to be decided, you know. I issue an order at the beginning of every week, specifying what must be done before Saturday night, when the party shall pass the night at Carlyle, and when at Humboldt, etc., and make it a rule to visit all work which requires attention, alternate days, myself."

" If I should write all my rules, you would tire very soon, — read a few through, please, and see if they suit you :

" No work shall be paid for which is not complete in every respect ; and a distance or height shall never be estimated by the eye in examining work.

" Every measurement of importance (as about bridge work) shall be made twice, starting from the other end the second time.

" Every number called out shall be repeated, and the signal — ' all right ' — made if correct.

" Two persons shall keep the record of instrument elevation in levelling, and check upon each other.

" The correction of an error must in no case be postponed, etc.

" There are, I think, fifty rules, and they make an undiscovered error an impossible occurrence."

He also said : " I postpone no work that I may do it on Sunday, and never call upon another to take one step upon that day when it can be dispensed with, only, when there is somewhat to do, I do it without hesitation ; and, having a clear conscience, calculate as correctly upon that day as upon another."

Judge Thacher, of Lawrence, attorney for the Leavenworth, Lawrence and Galveston Railway, writes : —

" I was present at one of the pay-days and was impressed with his (Mr. Firth's) scrupulous care in attending to the minutest details of the accounts. It was evident that the men placed implicit reliance upon his statements of what they had received from the company, and the amounts due them."

Mr. Firth said : " It is pleasant to deal with men who are satisfied with their earnings."

Their improvidence, however, was a great annoyance to him, and in regard to it, he wrote : " Having spent their lives on public works, they will linger in their old age in public charitable institutions."

Some of the laborers were Swedes, and, in his leisure moments, Mr. Firth was trying to learn to speak their language.

His purpose of doing six months' work in four, by industry and systematic management, was being accomplished at the expense of his own strength. June 22d, he wrote : " My head aches, not as a whole, but in sections, mainly in what I call the northeast corner (over the left eye)." In a characteristic manner he gave the reasons for " being sick at all."

" 1st. The pitifully low living (only rice, crackers, and eggs, which are fit for food).

" 2d. The nights are very damp and the days very hot ; in spite of the precautions I take, I feel the effect of this, and so do all my boys.

" 3d. The immediate occasion was over-exertion. I tired myself out and had no opportunity to rest, so that after a week's headache, the sickness has come. . . . I can defend the outer works, but when the enemy enters I am at his mercy."

June 26th, he announced himself "as well as ever"; but the disease was only subdued for a time, by force of will. He said afterwards, speaking of this time : "What is strangest to me is, that I should have had the strength to keep the fever at arm's-length so long. It would not do that I should have it until the day that I finished my work, and had matters so that I might leave them."

July 3d, the work was substantially completed. On that day he wrote : "I grow weaker and yellower every day. I can sit contented with my hands in my lap, hours together. . . . My boys are very full of attention, and do all they can for me. I will come home as a last resort ; but I will keep to my purpose unless chronic sickness is to be the price. It is my own good luck that sends this at the very properest time, while serious work is suspended and I lose nothing. . . . I couldn't help crying in reading your letter, though it seemed to me just as if some one else were doing so."

The home-letter advised his going to Lawrence to see a physician, and the next day he set out, thinking Mr. Chanute would give him a "leave of absence to recover." After an "awful journey" of thirty miles by stage, he reached Lawrence late at night. Fortunately, a Maine friend, whom he had not seen for five years, recognized his voice when he was groping about in the passage-way of the railway office, and took care of him, for he was too weak even to stand alone. He afterwards said of this friend, "he did more than a brother for me."

The next day, a physician pronounced his case to be typho-malarial fever, and he was taken to the house of the Rev. Mr. Starrett, where he found a home and kind care for a long time. The next ten days were a blank to him; but those about him, though strangers, were unremitting in their attentions. For a time his life wavered in the balance ; but July 15th, with trembling hand, he wrote : " My head is clear. . . . Lawrence friends are very kind, and ready to do anything for me. I had a delightful call from Mr. Chanute, who will send a line to you." Again : " I am a cat. I always drop on my feet, and it troubles me that you should have felt such anxiety. I think I could nowhere have received better care than here." And again : "I am sitting fully dressed, waiting to ride out with the doctor when he shall come."

A friend from Leavenworth went to see him, offering to escort him to Mr. Sargent's, in Chicago ; but neither his entreaties nor those of his own family could induce Mr. Firth to come away to recruit. " I should be ashamed to show my face in Boston," he said. " I will stand by my post while I have strength. . . . I will not retreat when it is not necessary. . . . Kansas caused my sickness and Kansas shall pay for it. . . . A morning-glory shoots up no faster than my strength increases." As soon as he was able to bear it, he had " a play of Shakespeare every day," — his nurse kindly reading for him. Nearly every day he wrote a letter home. Once he said : —

" The other night when I woke, Jupiter shone very brightly through the window, and while I sat up and watched him, my sickness and weakness seemed an idle loss of time in such a grand old universe. If a person had not one friend, how different recovery would be. . . . I feel happy, happy, happy, that I live, though I should have died quite unconsciously. . . . Did you ever lose the sense of water's freshness and know the exquisite joy of recovering it ? . . . Were you ever confined to a room so long that the air outside was intoxicating and the green of grass and trees a delicious treat ?" He thus wrote to his grandmother : " Rest assured, grandma, that one of my constitutional peculiarities is, that I never suffer any serious injury from disease or accident, and that in spite of all creation, I shall live until the work I was born to do is finished. I hope there is a considerable quantity of it."

The newspapers were now devoured with avidity. Mr. Firth took a great interest in the Franco-Prussian war, as the following extract shows : —

" I sincerely hope Napoleon is really dead ; but in that case, instead of the French army becoming demoralized, I should expect greater solidity under a new commander-in-chief ; and the war becoming one for the protection of France, and no longer for the aggrandizement of Louis Senior, and securing the succession of Louis Junior, all Frenchmen will come forward, and a popular government will inaugurate itself; that is, the present representative body must become supreme, and a national committee of safety be chosen, in whom the country will have faith." Much later he wrote on the same subject : " In our time we shall know a gay France no more. It seems her fate to teach the world lessons, and always to suffer from her own experiments."

His father passed the summer of 1870 in Europe. Mr. Firth was following his travels very closely, and by letters was constantly suggesting objects of interest or desirable routes.

As he began to think of work again, he learned that the

5

Lawrence, Leavenworth and Galveston road was at that time "checkmated"; but he said : " I shall not be thrown out of business, for Mr. Joy is my grand chief." August 23d, he was able to call upon Colonel Smith, who had also been ill with a fever. Though the construction on the road was discontinued, that gentleman gave him some office work which well suited his convalescence. He could apply himself but a few hours each day at first, but he lengthened the time with his increasing strength. August 28th, he wrote : —

" My map-work has become very pleasant. My only companion in the office is Captain Strong. As the work of neither is hindered by the wagging of tongues, we dis·cuss, predict, and combine all the facts we have learned from different sources. I only fear that more important service may call me away."

The call came in this form.

" KANSAS CITY, Sept. 3d.
" C. C. SMITH, or F. R. FIRTH : —

" I want Mr. Firth to go to Atchison to take charge of a road there. When can he be spared and get ready ?

"O. CHANUTE."

Enclosing a copy of the above, Mr. Firth wrote : " Just after the telegraph had brought to-day's glorious news of McMahon's surrender, the enclosed dispatch came to me. If I had only learned in the same way, that father arrived safely to-day, it could have done little more. . . . I leave in Lawrence many excellent friends and pleasant associations. Think of living beside the Missouri and among hills ! but you have n't been familiar with stagnant creeks and barren flats. I shall enjoy it heartily."

The highlands were as delightful as he anticipated, though, with the new duties of the next few months, he had scarcely time to look about him. As he expressed it, he wore blinders as part of his harness.

His position was that of resident engineer, Mr. Chanute being his chief. The history of the road with which he was connected, is thus given by the "Chicago Railway Review," of Oct. 5, 1871. "With the determination of late so characteristic of these 'rival' towns to become 'railway centres,' Atchison determined at any rate to secure in her own behalf a line in which she saw promise of fame and fortune. A half-score of her public-spirited citizens undertook the construction of a road north, under the name of the Atchison and Nebraska City. This was in 1869. Atchison County voted $150,000, and Doniphan County $150,000 in bonds, to the enterprise. The few thousand dollars of money needed to organize the company was supplied by the citizens above referred to, and with the proceeds of the bonds, grading was completed to the State line (Nebraska), thirty-eight miles. Being unable to prosecute the work, negotiations were entered into with different parties, which finally resulted in the transfer of the franchises of the company to Mr. Joy, who reorganized the company under the name of the Atchison and Nebraska." The section of country through which the route of the railway lay, was one of the first settled portions of Kansas.

Mr. Chanute writes : —

"The condition of the work on the Atchison and Nebraska Railroad, when he (Mr. Firth) took charge of it, was about as bad as it could be. The grading had been wretchedly done, the .cuts were not taken out to grade, the embankments were too narrow, in many cases, to lay the track at all, some of them were washed away altogether ; so, on a line which was said to be completed, we had to keep a large force ahead of the track-layers to repair the road-bed, so that it might be used. The ties were delivered in insufficient quantities at inaccessible places, were of bad timber, bad size, and badly made. The bridges were simply unsafe. Almost all of them had to be taken down, thrown away, and new ones built in their stead, before we laid the track."

September 17th, Mr. Firth wrote : —

" Already the new atmosphere of the class of people with whom I have to deal, makes itself felt. I have to do with employers of labor instead of laborers, and shall learn and gain by the improvement in a hundred ways." . . .

The first days were occupied in active preparations for track-laying. " I have been up and down and round about," he wrote, "looking for and at wood," and later, he was "unloading iron by moonlight." The articles sent for did not come as soon as he wished, and it was " without frogs and fish-plates " that the work was finally begun. It progressed well, however, and October 30th he wrote : " I have been in the way of issuing to every foreman, conductor, etc., etc., a plan in detail, on the morning of each day, the business of one dovetailing into the appointments of another, so that most could be accomplished with least loss of time. I have succeeded completely in such arrangements, and have operated two trains, and employed one hundred and forty men, graders, trackmen, carpenters, etc., besides doing a little freight business, laying ahead one half mile of track a day, hauling all supplies for track-laying, without clashing or serious accident."

His enthusiasm remained as fresh as ever. "You would like to see the first crossing of a bridge," he wrote. "The carpenters, graders, and trackmen crowded together, the cars and locomotive waiting the signal to run on and test it, then the careful feeling of it, as the train slowly moves forward and rests upon it. It is always a joyful feeling to see the locomotive across the stream one never crossed before."

Even the accidents were not without interest. "This wrecking business," he wrote, "affords excellent occasion for contrivance, and is on that account exciting and advantageous."

Early in November, the grading necessary to prepare for the steam-transfer across the Missouri River, at Atchison, was begun, adding another to Mr. Firth's "rather numerous pleasures and anxieties." In connection with this ferry, he made a survey and topographical map of the river, which was subsequently used in locating and letting the contract for the proposed bridge.

The first passenger train on the Atchison and Nebraska began to run as far as Doniphan, six miles, November 28th, on which occasion Mr. Firth wrote : "We can run with perfect safety twenty-five miles an hour, new as the road is." At Christmas time they had reached Fanning (twenty-three miles from Atchison). "Christmas," he said "is merry, and so is every day which leaves its mark in added improvement."

The laying of iron began September 22, 1870, and on the first of January, 1871, trains were running to White

Cloud. The Boston "Advertiser," of January 13th, contained the following : —

"Late Kansas papers give a glowing account of the opening of the Atchison and Nebraska Railroad to White Cloud, a distance of thirty-five and a half miles from Atchison. The party on the occasion had the judges, municipal officers of Atchison, and other citizens of influence. The Atchison and Nebraska Railroad is progressing beyond White Cloud, and will yet be continued to Lincoln, the capital of Nebraska. It is one of the 'Joy roads,' as they are called at the West, and so is sure of completion, and of having the work done in a creditable way. Its resident engineer is Mr. F. R. Firth, under whom it is being built and who is acting superintendent of the part already opened, Mr. Chanute being engineer in chief. Mr. Firth is a young man of good Massachusetts stock, of rare general ability, and superior qualifications for the profession of his choice. He is a graduate of the Institute of Technology. His rapid promotion, and the compliments he has received in other ways, have not surprised his friends here."

Mr. Chanute writes : " Mr. Firth had full charge of the construction of the work, my own visits not having averaged more than once a month after the first organization had been perfected. The track reached the State line of Nebraska in January, 1871, and he had done so well that Mr. Joy made him acting superintendent."

He now had greater responsibility than ever before. He wrote : " I pay a round price in care for the honor of being in sole charge of the work. I am eating, drinking, sleeping, and absorbing railway through my pores. . . . I am drifting far behind the times, and when I see you shall

be entirely ignorant of all the familiar people and events
of two years past."

A letter of January 15th said: "Now that construction
is ended for the time, another class of duties comes upon
me, that of retrenching expenses and making the road
begin to pay the $125,000 which I have spent upon it
already, entirely apart from the $400,000, or thereabouts,
which our material for track-laying cost." He adds: "I
am even called up in the night, occasionally, like a real
superintendent, though it all seems like play. . . . I do
like to try and realize how fortunate I have been. I know
that in many respects I am not wholly fitted for my position. I think that lack of experience, more than anything else, is at fault, and am trying my best to become
an old head."

He was constantly planning to increase the income of
the road, — at one time busied about procuring a mail
contract, and at another changing the time of trains, in
order thus to secure more travel.

In November he had written : " I have kept all our earnings in an envelope, and have about $18 against an expen-
diture of more than $150,000."

Writing to Mr. Chanute in January, he said : " The one
thing I wish more than any other, is to be able to send
money to Mr. Joy, as we shall do in no very long time."
Their earnings were then about $150 per day.

Notwithstanding his hopes, February 4th, he wrote: " I
have felt almost sick with anxiety, because I was notified
to spend no more money until Mr. Joy should visit the
road, and I knew that without continuing to repair, we
should kill some of our passengers and gain a bad reputa-

tion. I had decided to have nothing more to do with the road unless I could be free to make it safe and thoroughly good. All that concern is over, and I can sleep quietly, for my king, Mr. Joy, said yesterday, ' Everything is going on just as I wish.' I am doing as good work as I can, and as economically as I know how to do it."

At this time he was constantly receiving cautions about overworking, both from friends at home and from those about him. Mr. Rice (who had been on the Fort Scott road), says : " When I came up to Atchison, Mr. Firth was resident engineer and had just commenced track-laying. I never saw a person work so hard in all my life as he did. He seemed to think if he did not attend to everything himself, it would not be done as it ought to be. I remember one night Mr. Twichell, of Boston, came up to the office. It was about eleven o'clock. Mr. Firth was very busy posting up his books. Mr. Twichell begged and entreated him not to work so hard. He said the company were able to hire men to do the work. Mr. Firth said, ' I know that ; but it is only amusement for me ; and besides, when I do it myself, I know that it is finished and correct.' "

The reward of his labors was slow in coming. In March he wrote : " Every interest of the little road has become so personal a matter to me, that my sleep o' nights is good or bad, according to the day's receipts ; and when a train has failed to arrive, I have for a couple of hours been unable to read or write, with no desire to talk. . . . We never have twenty passengers upon a train, and in the matter of freight, I try to think that every week we carry more. Full or empty, though, my trains are safe." And again : " Poor No. 2 [locomotive] lies idle and dusty on a side track with no work to do ; but, though we receive little, we spend much."

One constant source of expense was the encroachment of the river upon the road-bed. Month after month Mr. Firth was obliged to carry on a struggle with the Missouri, an antagonist for whom he had a respect and liking, however. The Mississippi seemed to him a very stupid and spiritless creature, not to compare with his neighbor and enemy, the "Great Muddy." " The current connects one with all the world," he said, "and it is a daily pleasure to be beside the strong, far-coming, far-going stream ; an excellent means in some obscure way of bringing one to the point and keeping one uneasy." Uneasy it certainly kept them, in more senses than one. April 17th, Mr. Firth wrote : —

" In the mountains, two thousand miles away, the snow melted rapidly, and up came the Missouri, seven feet, and rolled and roared, and tore down its banks, and bullied us in half a dozen places ; but we were not frightened, and now the old fellow is in former limits, narrow and rapid and dirty, his broad bars offensive with the black mud just plastered over them. . . . Until you hear and see banks falling in, hour by hour, and many times in an hour, you will hardly realize what a power this river has to come out of its course."

It was not always that their enemy let them off so easily as on this occasion. In a letter to Mr. Chanute, written later in the season, Mr. Firth says : " Friday morning, the river, by a sudden change, commenced cutting in towards our line furiously, above Iowa Point. We fought, and are still fighting, with the largest trees we can handle, but can only hope to hold the present line long enough to construct one upon a new location which I have already chosen. We could not afford to attempt to resist the whole river which is now upon us, and the new line, although 6,000 feet long, will be cheaply constructed. If we can possibly hold the present line, I shall ; but if it is certain that we cannot, I shall not hesitate to build the new line, which I can do in very quick time."

In spite of all efforts, the river finally " got the best of Mr. Clark, the road-master," and the proposed change had to be made. On two other occasions the river cut away the track, and they had to "pick up and move." February 24th, 1871, Mr. Firth wrote to Mr. Chanute : " The road-bed for two hundred feet has settled and slid from under the track. This morning it was four feet below grade." By using " all the rock on hand at Iowa Point," a solid footing was secured, and trains were running as usual the next day. The sliding bluffs which the road skirted for a considerable distance, caused them much trouble. Mr. Firth was continually driven to devise expedients for keeping the road-bed in order ; and, indeed, it was only by great vigilance that trains were run over it in safety during the first year.

In May, we find him still going on with his usual work, having decided, by the advice of Mr. Chanute, and other friends, to retain his position on the road, and to give up the opportunity which he might have had, of building the bridge over the Kansas River, at Lawrence.

May 1st, he wrote: "I find the cares greater than the satisfaction, with many things to do, and limited means of accomplishing what is necessary. Our business is lighter than ever."

May 5th, the first rail was laid in Nebraska, Col. Abell, president of the road, driving the first spike. During this month Mr. Firth received his appointment as superintendent, and May 22d he said : " I have arranged to spend three days as superintendent in Kansas, and four as engineer in Nebraska." Having received from his father, to whom he had sent for railroad documents, a report of the Boston & Albany Railroad, he wrote : " By playing with blunt ones, I shall gain the skill for handling edged tools, and then I'll compete with you in total number of trains, number and speed of express trains, freedom from accident, etc., etc."

Though baffled and hampered in some respects, in others he was able to carry out his ideas in a satisfactory manner. In regard to some new stations which he was having built, he wrote : " The problem was, to combine freight and passenger houses in one. I adopted passenger-house architecture for passenger part, and freight for freight. The passenger part is towards the town. The building looks very well. The object was, economical use of room and general handiness for use, not beauty. I put a spreading roof around passenger part, but did not make a flaring roof upon the freight ; using the space rather for merchandise. At all events, it is the only one of its kind, but I hope and trust it will be copied." Another experiment in a different direction proved also quite successful. April 7th, he wrote : " My first theatre train, last evening, was an entire success. I think our gross receipts are one hundred and twenty-five dollars."

And again, in July : " We are dispensing with contractors almost wholly, laying our own tracks, building our own depots, putting up our tanks, turn-tables, etc., and shall keep our own boarding-train, boarding the men ourselves. A company with its men properly chosen, can do all these things, cheaply and honestly. . . . This is rather novel practice here in the West, and I am working very carefully, but with marked success so far. We have laid our track for less than four hundred dollars a mile, and can run thirty miles an hour upon this bran-new track, with safety, and do so."

Mr. Chanute, speaking of Mr. Firth's dispensing with contract work, says : " This did not apply to grading and general railroad building. . . . When he first proposed the plan, I opposed it. . . . I consented, however, to his trying the experiment, and found to my surprise that he gave the work such close attention, that he actually did it cheaper than it could be contracted at. This, however, was partly due to the shortness of his road, which enabled him to give close supervision to details ; but most of the saving was undoubtedly due to his talent for organizing and directing."

.One of the greatest pleasures connected with his present position, was the opportunity it gave him for helping others. He wrote his friends that he was now able to " start any deserving and valuable men" who wished to follow his profession. He would like, he said, " men whom he could consider as rivals as well as companions." Accordingly, several persons went out to him at different times. To one of them he thus wrote : —

" I know your cousin, and, if I am not mistaken, I have

met you. At all events, every engineer is a friend of who-
ever practises, or desires to practise, the profession. The
West is, beyond question, the best school for practice, on
account of the rapidity with which work is done, and, consequently, the great variety of difficulties one learns to
encounter in a short time, and the certainty of advancement when deserved. The call for engineers, for ten
years, has been beyond the supply, and men nowise quali-
fied for the duties style themselves engineers, and waste
a great deal of money for their employers. Every man
who proves himself energetic, industrious, accurate, and
responsible, can gain a position of trust in as many months
here as he would require years in the East. But no step
must be neglected in working one's way forward. You
must know the duties of every man under your direction
from experience, and no matter how much theory a man
may have, when he begins practice, he must carry an axe
or a level rod, put up with rough fare, and camp in strange
company. The first year is always a hard one, and one
must be prepared to go wet or dry, sick or hungry, as the
case may be, and make the best of it. It would be difficult to find an opening at once, in a place of trust, even in
the West, but it is easy to find employment as a common
hand. I did so when I came here, and roughed it for ten
months under canvas, then lived in a shanty, then in a
little brick house, and now have offices lighted with gas,
etc. I can only speak to you, of course, from my own
experience, but am sure that I would do the same thing
again, and advise you to make up your mind to begin at
the bottom and work your way forward. . . . Engineering
is a satisfactory, healthy profession, and educates every

faculty a man has ; but the price to be paid is an unsettled life, and continual change of friends and surroundings."

Mr. Firth afterwards said, speaking of a young engineer who had become a little impatient of "the slow, hardening process which makes men out of boys," "You know I once thought I was n't appreciated, and that the hill was rolling over a trifle faster than I climbed up."

Upon the Atchison and Nebraska Road, Mr. Firth had found already some of his former companions, and others came by his invitation. He wrote in October, 1871 : —

"Many old Fort Scott men are here, and it is pleasant to have a track-layer or a spiker allude to having seen me before."

Two of the surveying party, to which he first belonged, now joined him, of one of whom Mr. Firth wrote : —

"It was Mr. Holmes who permitted me to use the level, so that I was able to prove my capacity to use an instrument."

He soon had about him a body of men in whom he took great pride and satisfaction. March 5th, he wrote : —

"I think we have the virtues of a new road with the steadiness of an old one." And again : "I never knew men so much interested in the welfare of each other, and so enthusiastic for the progress of the work, as the present organization. By meeting every man three times a week upon his work, one can cheer, encourage, and rally them, and, without hurrying, hasten matters."

In June he said : "I have a set of men here, selected from the dozens and fifties who have applied, and not a second-rate one among them. Every one remarks the harmony with which my men, in all departments, co-operate, and I have the perfect satisfaction of knowing that whatever directions are given will be fulfilled to the letter, and that every man will do his duty cheerfully, and feel proud to do it well. It is a pleasure to have such a corps at command, and I would not exchange them for father's." And again: "I used to feel anxious, but now I don't know what that is. The trains are never behind time ; no man ever fails to accomplish what he is set to do upon the day named ; and such a thing as a dispute, or soreness, or ill-feeling among the men, is unknown.

In July, he wrote: "I might leave the road to-morrow morning for a week, confident that every movement would be made according to plan, although every day requires a different programme, and there are three trains to be kept simultaneously in motion upon a single-track road, fifty miles long, and without a telegraph line."

His feeling for his associates constantly appears in his letters. In the latter part of the year 1871, he wrote : " I have men who will work night or day, in storm or fair weather, — Sundays, holidays, and all, if necessary ; who would rather lose a hand than have an accident happen ; and who care more for the advantage of the road than for their own. . . . I never hear swearing or foul language among our men ; not because they are silent when I am near, but because I have n't a profane man."

His men justified the confidence he placed in them. One of them wrote to him : "As you say you will not forget my interest, I will look well to that of the company, and still continue to make your interest my own."

Another, writing to thank Mr. Firth for an extra sum of money sent him with his month's wages. said, apropos

of a rumor that some one was to take his place : " If that
is the case, I assure you I will do everything in my power
to assist him as long as it is to your interest. Outside of
that, I have none on the Atchison and Nebraska Railway.
Do not hesitate to give charge to Mr. ——, or any other man,
if you think he can do better for you than I have. I shall
always feel sure of your friendship, no matter how things
go. That is all I ask for past services, — that belongs to
me." Another wrote in 1872 : " I do not know anything,
sir, that would give me more pain than I would feel if I
were to do any act that would justly forfeit your esteem.
I feel that I would be wanting in the commonest feelings
of humanity if I did not at all times both entertain and
express for you the highest regard as an associate, and my
entire esteem as a man."

There was a tenderness in the sentiment which Mr.
Firth inspired in those in his employ. For example, Mr.
—— wrote : " It has occurred to me that my remarks
this morning might have a tendency to injure your feelings. . . . Indeed, so far as I am individually concerned,
I wish to place on record that I never dealt with any man
that seemed to wish to do more right than yourself."

Mr. B., writing of injury done by a gale, said : " I hope
you will not worry over this thing, for I assure you it wor-
ries me very much." Another expresses himself as follows : " I trust that I may do nothing, in your absence or
when you are here, which will make you unhappy for a
single moment."

One who had left the Atchison and Nebraska, wrote to
Mr. Firth : " It is a source of regret to me that I ever
resigned my position under yourself." Another says :

"There were once or twice rumors started that Mr. Firth was going to resign. I don't think there was a man on the road but what said he hoped he would not leave, and if he did, he would follow him to whatever road he went."

The idea of building railroads in Japan was very attractive to Mr. Firth, and he often talked of going there sometime. He wrote: "I have a corps of men all ready to go with me, and we often anticipate the expedition."

"I want you to know my men," he said, when his father thought of coming to visit him. His wish has been fulfilled, since his own work was done, and the sympathy of these faithful friends has been very precious to the family in their affliction.

With such a corps, it is no wonder that Mr. Firth could say, as he did in June, 1871 : "Blue days of old A. & N. are past. We shall make a good record, whether any one reads it or not." And in July : "The Atchison and Nebraska will probably be no more than self-supporting for a year ; but in three years, it will begin to repay its capital. . . . My instructions when I came were to make it a third-class road. I made it second-class, and now, after a little, I shall advance the standard to first-class. . . . It will be three years in becoming first-class, but I have that always in view, and now know that the business will authorize me."

No pains were spared to reach the proposed standard as nearly, and as early as the means at his command would permit, and that these efforts were appreciated, is shown by favorable mention in the various local papers. One of them says : —

"We pronounce this road the best and smoothest new

6

road over which we ever passed ;" and a series of resolutions passed by a company of excursionists, particularly mentions the "smoothness of the road-bed, and
the excellence of the road's equipments." As a part of
these, we find noticed two handsome and substantial
twelve-wheeled passenger-cars, furnished with the Miller
coupling and a patent brake, and "patent ventilators, and
smoke and cinder guards," these carriages having been
recently manufactured for the company, and added to their
rolling stock. Mr. Firth said : —

"Our engines are beauties, except the 'Antelope,' and
she looks like an old lady dressed as a modern belle."

In August, he wrote : "I have not drawn the three
thousand [salary], because I do not think the road can well
afford it ; but whenever I wish, I can have it, and as soon
as I can afford it (officially), I shall take it (personally).

But in September, he said, showing how business had
been improving during the summer: "I'm drawing my
two hundred and fifty dollars a month, now ;" and in August the road's receipts averaged two hundred and fifty
dollars a day.

Work was all the time being pushed on at "the front."
Mr. Firth mentioned, in a letter written July 1st, that
they had laid three quarters of a mile of track in three
hours and a half.

Early in the season Mr. Firth had begun a series of
excursions which lasted late into the autumn. They were
sometimes free, or for half fares, as on occasion of picnic
parties or of opening the road to a new point ; some were
made from Atchison to the Nebraska towns, others from
Rulo, Falls City, etc., to Atchison ; thus promoting pleas-

ant, mutual relations between the Kansas and Nebraska portions of the road. The company, on such occasions, generally resolved itself into a meeting and passed resolutions, after the American fashion, showing a very cordial feeling to the road and towards their neighbors. Mr. Firth himself was usually passing from car to car on the way, taking a general care, and ready to answer all questions.

On the 24th of June occurred a great masonic picnic, the largest of the season, of which occasion Mr. Firth was very glad to write that the railway company had "handled between seven and eight hundred people without the least accident." The train was run as far as the new bridge, two hundred and fifty-five feet in length, over the Nemaha, in order to allow the passengers to examine the structure, and was then backed a mile or more to the picnic ground. Mr. Firth mentioned the picturesque effect of "a thousand people in bright-colored holiday dress, Indians on the outskirts of the party," while in the background was seen the grove, and "Old Muddy, with a smile on his dirty face."

On the 4th of July, a train for the first time passed over the Nemaha bridge (first crossing), and the event was celebrated by a small excursion party to Rulo and Falls City.

The railway company had purchased a picnic ground, and during the summer were arranging and making it more attractive and convenient. Late in November, Mr. Firth wrote : —

"Our excursion Thursday was the success of the season. It was one of the dreariest, stormiest days of all the year ; but from St. Joseph, Leavenworth, and Atchison together, we had two hundred people, ladies and gentlemen, and such a gay time, I think, was never seen in cars. Singing, speaking, waltzing in the aisles, music of the quadrille band, and all sorts of games." On such a day the grove was, of course, out of the question, and a table was spread under cover.

Mr. Firth was now universally known as "Major," a title which had been first given him by one of the newspapers, and which ever after clung to him, in spite of his often expressed objection to it.

In September, 1871, he was made Chief Engineer, as well as Superintendent of the Atchison and Nebraska, Mr. Chanute retiring from the position in order to become Superintendent of the Leavenworth, Lawrence and Galveston railway. The two gentlemen parted with the most cordial regard on both sides. Indeed, the younger had an especially strong feeling for his chief, of whom he spoke as "one of my models."

The Atchison and Nebraska road now owned six locomotives, but still needed a telegraph line, which Mr. Firth hoped to have before the end of the season.

He constantly called the attention of the public to the road by means of communications adressed to various papers.

The progress of the railway during the summer is stated in a letter written by him to the "Railroad Gazette," from which the following is an extract:—

"The road crosses the St. Joseph and Denver City railroad at Troy Junction, sixteen miles west of St. Joseph, and passes through Doniphan, Troy, Highland, Iowa Point, and White Cloud. In the spring, Mr. Joy purchased of the Burlington and Southwestern Railway Company, their property in the Nemaha valley, with the ten miles of track

already laid from Rulo west, but never used. The location of the Burlington and Southwestern in Nebraska had
been completed to Humboldt, thirty-three miles from
Rulo, the track laid to a point two miles east of Falls
City, and the grading nearly finished as far as Humboldt.
No bridging, however, had been done west of Falls City.
During April, May, and June, the six and a half miles of
grading necessary to connect the original Atchison, Nebraska, and State Line with the Burlington and Southwestern track, were completed, and July 4th, the road was
open to Falls City, county seat of Richardson County.
Since that time the grading to Humboldt has been completed, grading nine miles farther nearly finished, a new
location of line, two miles in length (made necessary by
the inroad of the Missouri between Iowa Point and White
Cloud), graded and finished, and ten miles of track laid on
main line. Want of iron delayed us nearly three weeks.
From State Line, north, the work is thoroughly done ;
bridging substantial, ditching sufficient, and, though not
expensive, it is a good road-bed, and such as the present
business warrants. With increasing business, the standard can be raised without the loss of any work already
done. We use Howe truss bridges, and lay a fifty-pound
rail (Cambria Works), with first-class ties, build substantial, creditable stations, and have equipment which will
compare well with that of any road west of the Mississippi,
being of the same charac.er with that of other 'Joy'
roads, — a well-known standard.

"The road is being steadily improved between Atchison
and State Line, bridges replaced, etc., and the condition
of the track is excellent. At Rulo, the line of the road

leaves the Missouri and takes a northwesterly course up the valley of the great Nemaha, into the rich, unpublished country, Southern Nebraska, through land which would warrant any statement I could make in its praise. This is the first road to lay open to settlement this truly beautiful section, and it will be our pleasure and duty to aid in its development. We shall offer every facility to immigration, and shall co-operate with the land owners, agents, town companies, etc., in bringing these lands into notice. Do not understand me that the country is unsettled; by no means. Falls City, Rulo, and Salem are well-built, well-to-do, growing places, and there are many large, finely improved farms, but the population is very small in comparison with the land's capacity. Only its previous inaccessibility, and the immediate neighborhood of so well ventilated [*i. e.* widely advertised] a country as Southern Kansas, has deprived it of its due share of public attention. Nebraska has had no domestic troubles to give it notoriety, and has lost the consequent advantages.

"The objective point of one branch of our line is Lincoln, Nebraska. Of another, some point upon the Union Pacific Railroad not determined. . . . The lands of Southern Nebraska are cheap, accessible, and as good as the best. The especial peculiarity of the country is that *all the land is good.* The best land here is no better than the best land elsewhere, of course; but it is not often, so far as our knowledge of the West goes, that one can find soil almost uniformly rich, and the slopes so flat that the uplands bear crops almost as well as the bottoms. The climate is better suited to northern people than that of more southern places, and the present settlers are not 'squatters,' but hard-working farmers, who have something to show for their labor."

In accordance with the views above expressed, Mr. Firth issued a circular of invitation for a meeting to be held in the Nemaha Grove, September 28th, saying that the time had come for "organized co-operation to draw the attention of farmers, stock raisers, emigrants, — all but speculators, — to a country from which no man can return disappointed," and stating that the railway company wished to join with the land owners in order to establish a "land office at which those looking for farms and homes might receive full and correct information." At the close of the circular Mr. Firth said : "Our Nebraska friends will meet with this in view ; but others from abroad will be expected only to examine our new road, picnic with us, and condemn the land they will see if they can conscientiously."

In response to this call, a convention was held at the appointed place and time, by the "merchants, business men and farmers of Southern Nebraska and Northern Kansas," the company being guests of Mr. Firth. After dinner, the meeting was called to order, and speeches were made by Hon. S. C. Pomeroy and General B. F. String-fellow, relative to the advantages of that section of the country and the best means of developing it. The "modest Major" followed with a brief address, explaining the purposes of the convention and pledging the hearty aid of the Atchison and Nebraska, whose interests, he said, though itself owning no land, were identical with those of the people of Southern Nebraska. A committee appointed for the purpose met and reported a constitution and by-laws for the "Southern Nebraska Emigrant Society"; officers were elected, Mr. J. F. Gardner, of Falls City, being president, and Mr. F. R. Firth one of the directors, and resolutions were offered, advising that the Nemaha Valley should be systematically advertised, and that proper arrangements should be made for directing emigration thither. Business completed, the party, after partaking of a supper ordered by their host, at White Cloud, returned to Atchison. Soon after, a large poster was printed, by order of Mr. Firth, announcing to the public that Southern Nebraska was open to immigration, setting forth the advantages of the fertile valley, "not the cheapest land, but the best," and stating that farm produce could be shipped to St. Louis and Chicago without change of cars. Acting upon his strong faith in the value of Nemaha land, Mr. Firth himself purchased a farm on the line of his road. At one time he had in his office an ear of Nebraska corn "weighing one pound, eight and a half ounces, and containing 1,254 grains."

The autumn of 1871 was so busy a time that he was obliged to give up a proposed visit to Boston ; but late in November he wrote : "Winter has set in in dead earnest and in the old-fashioned New-England way." Consequently construction was discontinued. The road had reached Table Rock, eighty-four miles from Atchison, which point remained its terminus for the winter.

Mr. Firth still found a little work to do, however. December 3d, he wrote : "I have been very busy for three days, running the steam-transfer here. The river fell, and the crossing of cars stopped ; and as the Kansas City, St. Joseph, and Council Bluffs folks made no effort to put it again in order, I volunteered to do so if they would furnish me all the men and material I wanted. This they did, and I continue in charge of the ferry."

Mr. Firth's activity was a marvel to all who knew him. Thus, one of his letters said : " During the week I have walked fifty miles, ridden on horseback, in stage, private conveyance, freight-cars, passenger-cars, and locomotives. Spent one moonlight evening on top of a freight-train, went bathing in the Missouri, and have had a free-and-easy week." Once, when a slight accident happened to a train on which he was riding, he immediately started for Atchison on a hand-car, assisting to propel it himself, and on arriving, set out again with aid for the train. While " prospecting " for further extension, he often went on long jaunts. For example : " From 6.30 this morning until eight this evening (save an hour's snoozing), I have been on horseback. Wyatt and I have been reconnoitring the country between here and Lawrence." Again, in a letter of September, 1871 : " Wednesday afternoon, went up the road in my woollens, and had one of those long walking and riding tours at the front. Mr. Holmes and I rode on the prairie until nearly eleven P. M., slept in a little farm-house, and at six yesterday I was here again, and rather tired. All our work goes well, — so well one almost fears."

During the winter of 1871–2, he walked through to Lincoln (from Table Rock), when he had to stop on the road and thaw the frost out of his face. In March, 1872, he wrote : " Made journey to the end of track, camped out one night, and delivered a speech more than an hour long in a crowded school-house, which a single small candle very feebly illuminated."

One of his men says: "I don't think anything ever transpired on the road but what he knew about it." His power of apparently being at all points at once was regarded by his men as something almost supernatural. "It is lonely upon the road now," said a brakeman, after the accident; "we never knew when the Major would come out from behind a bush and signal us to whistl ' brakes and take him on."

Mr. Firth was in the habit of passing over and observing other roads as well as his own. From Falls City, he wrote Tuesday, October 24, 1871 : " Since I left Atchison, last Thursday, at ten A. M., I have travelled about fifteen hundred miles, and spent some hours at Lincoln, Chicago, Burlington, and Galesburg ; rode altogether two hundred miles upon four different engines equipped with the Westinghaus brake, for the purpose of becoming familiar with it."

The following illustrates the rapidity with which he travelled: " I was at the Massasoit (Atchison), at midnight last night, having, since two P. M., been in four States. . . . Saturday, P. M., I took tea in Missouri, spent the evening in Kansas, slept half the night in Missouri, woke in Iowa, eat breakfast in Nebraska, and saw the sun set in Iowa." And again : " Had to go to St. Louis, and so made a call at Chicago."

Mr. Firth's note-books of 1870–71 contain some fragmentary jottings of interest, such as the following : " The object of ballasting is to make a firm, undisturbed road-bed ; this it does in virtue of its own solid compactness, and by its perfect drainage. It is paid by the lessening of running expenses, by the preservation of unhurt iron,

by the prevention of decay in ties. . . . A railway company might produce its own ties by locust or black-walnut
trees planted by the road-side, allowing 500 to the acre ;
upon a strip 25 feet wide, one mile long, there would be
(3.03 acres) 1,515 trees ; 2,600 ties needed per mile. Upon
the inside of curves they could not be permitted. (The
right of way, 100 feet wide, measures 12.12 acres per
mile.)" The same book contains a suggestion that the
government should collect and preserve the results of
railway surveys, which, he said, being made with a view
to actual, expensive construction, were taken in great
detail. He thought that while the work was fresh, it was
the proper time to inaugurate such a system as would
render at once available "an immense amount of topographical information, now buried in unconnected data."

The memoranda continue : " It is an American curse
that men are all impatient for the opportunity to do what
they cannot do. . . .

" An excitable man is an expensive one.

" If you distrust a man, come upon him before the time
appointed.

" Do not praise unfinished work.

" My experience convinces me that it would be well to
enroll men, regularly enlist them, for railway service, letting
them subscribe to a contract which should be short and
distinct, and the punishment for violating it, immediate
dismissal. First, obedience to orders. Second, temperance
and good behavior. Third, to do whatever the interests
of the company demanded, when directed. Fourth, to
make no claim for extra service, or irregular service.
—although gratuities may advantageously be bestowed

" Men should only be responsible directly to one person.

" Pay no attention to trivial errors of an assistant. Never ask a man to do what you cannot and would not do yourself.

" It is not virtue to want ambition.

" Every man should keep a horse, and learn how food can affect immediately every physical action.

" Two hours at some future day are worth three now ; do I not increase in value? why then postpone?

" Never be without occupation for intervals.

" A peculiarly fitting time of day for each ceremony : funeral at sunset ; marriage in morning ; execution, — midnight ; business contract at midday."

One can fancy that the note, "Social improvements which money could accomplish," pointed to Mr. Firth's intention to make a fortune early, and retire from his profession. The following, also, may have been a suggestion for the occupation of some future leisure hours.

" Books which should be written : Railway Accidents, — causes, with a view to prevention."

We add a few more extracts : —

" *Maxims.*

" Speak as little as possible.

"Say nothing which will have no interest an hour hence.

" Believe nothing which will injure your friend's good name ; my friend against twenty accusers.

" The highest attainment ; the power to be idle, and content to divert yourself from an absorbing pursuit."

The power of withdrawal from work was one which he

had lately been acquiring, as during the past summer he had had more "leisure to cultivate society," for which his inclination, also, had been growing. He wrote, in the autumn of 1871: "I am only in this respect changed, that I feel no hesitation in speaking to man, woman, or child to whom I have anything to say and pay no regard to what people will think, in doing what I think is best. . . . . With the large appreciation I now have of the necessary mutual dependence of people for kindly, friendly offices, and the criminal wrong-headedness of isolation, there is no danger of becoming a misanthrope, or a voluntary prisoner."

In September, with a friend, he entertained the whist club to which he belonged at his office, the latter made attractive by means of evergreens, flowers, photographs, and borrowed tables and chairs. After a leap-year ball, he wrote home that he should dance hereafter, at every ball he attended,—"a resolution I never really formed before."

A letter of February 2, 1872, said: "I spend an hour or more every evening, in visiting my friends, and forget the initials 'A. and N.' for a few hours."

At the homes, where he ever found a cordial welcome, he was a favorite with all, talking politics with the father, indulging in fun and repartee with the young people, and always ready to play with the children. He seldom made a call without leaving some reminder of himself, in the form of a book, a piece of music, or a magazine. In the neighboring cities he had social as well as business connections. Many of his private letters received during the past year were written in acknowledgment of favors which he had conferred on Kansas friends. One was found, thanking

him for sending home, with his debts paid, a young man
who had fallen into bad ways and company.

The Atchison and Nebraska railway passes through the
Indian Reserve, occupied by the Sacs and Foxes. In the
Quakers at the mission there Mr. Firth found warm
friends, often stopping to see them on his way up or down
the line. He also had pleasant relations with the Indians
themselves. He wrote : —

"The Indians made and sold us the best cross-ties I
ever saw ; " and again : " Saturday, being away, I missed
a call from six Iowa chiefs who came down with Mrs.
Lightfoot's Indian school in a car I had promised them
long ago. The chiefs expressed to Mr. Deitz, by inter-
preter, that they should feel honored by a visit from me,
and invited me to let them know when I would sit in council with them."

Of Mr. Firth's strong and steadily-growing feeling for
the West and Western people, it is hardly possible to say
too much. Letter after letter was written in the same
strain. For instance : —

"I wish Southern people knew Northerners as they are,
and I wish still more that Northerners knew Southern and
Western people, for they do not understand them, and cannot be just to them for lack of acquaintance with them.
The westernizing process has been very rapid with me for
the past six months, and I am sure I am none the worse
for it. . . . I have not changed my standard for judging of
people and things very radically in these few years, for to
become a Western man is to add to, not alter the Eastern
man." The whole-hearted work and ways of his daily companions were a constant delight to him. "Western young

men," he said " (if you choose to call them Western, they are as often English and German as Americans), give themselves to their work, having chosen it, and do not drop their tool because the clock strikes six, or allow an insult to their employers to pass without notice. . . . I know twenty men who would throw themselves under the wheels of a train to save a life, or would do just such manly, self-denying deeds as Bret Harte records, without taking a thought of its being more than an act of duty. There is a flavor to Western life, and a ring of true metal about real Western men, which has a charm for those who believe that human nature is not wholly bad, and that virtue is not conditional on grammatical speech."

In still another letter : " They decorate soldiers' graves in the West just as in the East. You must remember that it is all one country." Even the air, earth, and water of his new home came in for a share of his affections. In spite of a touch of the " chills " from which he had suffered in the autumn, he wrote home in November : " I am converted to the Kansas climate ; when it storms, little can be said for it ; but when it is fair, nothing can compare with it."

This admiration for the West included its railway men. He wrote : " I enjoy very much my extending and already somewhat extended railway acquaintance. I meet people continually whom I have never seen before, but have known by name, who have also heard of me, so we are friends from the beginning." When a new question arose, he often consulted his neighbors of older experience, the Superintendents of the Chicago, Burlington & Quincy, and Hannibal & St. Joseph Railroads, and, as he said, received from them "all the assistance " he ever asked.

Meanwhile, Mr. Firth himself was taking his rank among railway officials, and as a friend wrote of him, already had a " reputation well-established for economy of construction and management." He was popular, too, to an extent which surprised even his best friends. One of his associates writes : " Mr. Firth had a peculiar manner of talking, that to a stranger sounded overbearing. He always talked business in as few words as possible. I have heard quite a number say that when they first commenced talking with him, they thought he was almost impudent ; but after they got acquainted, they found him a perfect gentleman."

His slight, boyish figure was a surprise to those who had previously known him by reputation, and they were no less astonished at the readiness with which his mind grasped any subject or question brought before it, explaining the expression used by a Western paper, that he was " smart as lightning."

As he scorned everything like fawning, the regard of those with whom he was associated did not come as the result of any effort on his part, but was called forth by his real worth.

Mr. Firth's fairness in dealing, and his fidelity to his word, soon gained for him the honor and confidence of those living on the line of the railway.

One of the local papers said : " The officers and employees of the Atchison and Nebraska will do more to accommodate shippers and the travelling public, than any set of men we ever saw in charge of a railroad."

A Leavenworth paper alluded to the " debt of gratitude " due Mr. Firth, and the " Kansas Chief " (White

Cloud) said that he had "secured for the road the good-will of the entire country along the route."

He was, however, unwilling to resort to any schemes for the advancement of sectional interests, as is shown in the following extract from a letter written at the time when a neighboring road was plotting to further the interests of its terminal town : —

" This protective policy is opposed to the truest American ideas, for few men like to have it decided for them where they must buy and how they shall ship ; and in the West, more especially, the arbitrary closing of a channel is, as it should be, an unpopular action."

He was himself falling into Western ways of thinking.

" The West," he wrote, " is unequivocally Free Trade, and I cannot see how a man not interested in coal, iron, or salt, can conscientiously be otherwise."

With a mind full of railway projects and details, he still, as in former times, kept up an interest in the topics of the day, and did not forget that he was a citizen of the republic : " I consider my political life as dating from Grant's inaugural," he wrote, " and shall try to keep myself informed upon the problems and acts of government, as if I had a share in it."

He was " glad that Kansas led off on the XVth article " ; speaking of which, he said : " What we do write of and think of, is petty, trivial in comparison ; but for all that, we none the less feel the grand fact. This is a nation to fight for ; it is the freest country upon the face of the earth, God save it — with our help — while we may, and so long as none is freer."

That he was ready to give his help, was shown in his

7

relations to the colored people. A negro boy was employed
in the railway shops at Rulo. Until that time, no person of
his race had ever been allowed in the town, and the inno-
vation was followed by threats of violence ; but " Bostwick
secured six revolvers and let Rulo know that the boy
should remain."

, The colored people appreciated Mr. Firth's position re-
garding them, as was shown by a conversation which took
place in an Atchison street, while he was lying ill in his
room : —

"Are you any relation to Major Firth?" said a colored
man.

"I am his father."

"Let me shake hands with you. There is n't a black
man in Atchison who would n't die for Major Firth. He
was the first railway man to employ us. We all pray that
he may get well."

From time to time, friends at home sent Mr. Firth
accounts of the pleasures they were enjoying in theatre,
opera, and concert. " Thanks for the play-bills," he wrote ;
"I will have my revenge, and see better players than
Fechter and Seebach, and hear sweeter singers than
Nilsson, to my heart's content, in the next half century.
After the aspera we shall see stars, as the Kansas motto [*Ad
astra per aspera*], than which none is better, suggests."

He enjoyed seeing and hearing Nilsson, when for the
Christmas holidays he came to Boston which he had last
left in February, 1870. He had a very happy visit at home.
As one of his little cousins said, he never was so " jolly "
before. In fact, he had seemed for a long time to be growing younger in feeling, while he grew older in years, and

overcoming the reserve which had made him grave as a boy, his natural love of fun had free play. His friends heartily enjoyed his bright visit, little thinking that the gay good-by with which he left them was the last word that most of them were ever to hear from his lips.

During the winter, Mr. Firth prepared for distribution maps of the Atchison and Nebraska road and its connections, a copy of which, with some additions, is found at the close of this volume.

In February, 1872, through the newspapers, he called for bids from contractors for the grading of the road-bed from Sterling to Lincoln (both in Nebraska), a distance of thirty-five miles, and March 2d, an eighty-thousand-dollar contract was closed, and the work begun at once. The next day Mr. Firth wrote: "Vacation is really over." Again, March 26: "Our business is increasing at all points, and one must be dismal indeed who cannot feel cheered by the increasing prosperity of his road." April 9th: "Congratulate me on my first hundred miles of road completed;" and May 1st: "Our earnings upon the Atchison and Nebraska, this last month, amount to $15,000, and are, of course, increasing."

In the preceding March, Mr. O. E. Allen, of Northboro', Massachusetts, had come to Atchison with a letter from Mr. W. F. Weld, of Boston, asking Mr. Firth to initiate him into the railway service. Mr. Allen was a member of the senior class at Harvard College, but left study for work thus early, in order to become acclimatized before the summer.

He acted as clerk and general assistant for Mr. Firth, and there soon sprung up between the two young men a most devoted friendship.

Mr. Firth wrote: "Nothing since I came west has been so pleasant for me as the finding in Allen an intimate friend who likes to do everything I like to do, and dislikes what I dislike, and who is a hearty, wholesome fellow withal." In a letter written June 6th, but never mailed, he said: "Allen and I can find nothing to quarrel, or even disagree about; it is ludicrous to find ourselves saying the same thing in the very same words, as we sometimes do." Mr. Allen wrote: "Mr. Firth and I are like a pair of lovers." Their common taste for out-door exercise formed a bond of sympathy between them. In May, Mr. Firth wrote: "Sunday before last, Allen and I walked forty-eight miles, from Tecumseh to Lincoln, without being the worse for it."

Together the friends fitted up some lodgings in a new building opposite the railway offices in Atchison, and much enjoyed having a place they might call home. They selected their furniture with an eye to beauty as well as comfort; from their Eastern homes pictures and books were sent, and, leaving a piano until they could afford it, Mr. Firth was able to write: "Our rooms are all that we hoped, airy, comfortable, and home-like, — a great relief after four years of Arab life." May 25th, they had their house-warming and received their friends, little Pip, the dog whom they owned together, assisting his two masters in their duties as hosts. Their housekeeping received many compliments from the pleasant company assembled.

Among the objects which had been chosen for ornament or use, Mr. Firth particularly mentioned the bookcase, "a very good-looking fellow and excellent company." He had long relied on such society as these shelves now

ⱼffered. As may be seen from his letters during the
whole period of his Western life, he had been continually
receiving books, periodicals, and papers from his father,
and, as soon as he had a place in which to put them, he
sent for a collection which should make the foundation of
a library. " You may think my order a large one," he
said, " but you cannot know how hungry one gets for
book-case friends." In addition to his old companions,—
Marcus Aurelius, Shakespeare, Emerson, Motley, Buckle,
Tyndall, Thackeray, Reade, and many others, — he now
sent for a large number of books on different subjects, such
as books of reference, scientific works : Carlyle's French
Revolution and Hero Worship, Helps' writings, Plutarch's
Lives and Morals, Don Quixote, Goethe's novels, the
British Dramatists, Smith's Wealth of Nations, — " the
latest and best Oxford edition," — Redfield's Railway
Law, some of the old English and other poets, Unitarian
hymn-books, and the Church of England service. To this
order his father added some selections of his own, with
all of which Mr. Firth was much pleased. " What a hard-
looking set they 'll be," he wrote, " after going around the
world with me, full of dust of all lands, and stained with
water of all seas ; associated with friends, and restorers of
my life, whatever it may be, when it is passed."

He had always spoken in home letters of the books in
which he happened to be interested at the time, and liked
to exchange ideas and criticism with his correspondents.
"I have been reading the ' Virginians ' in a very leisurely
way, and have enjoyed the flavor of the olden time very
much, " — he said one day ; " I had really forgotten that
the port of Boston was closed and the custom-house

removed to Salem on account of the Boston tea-party."
And again : " I open Emerson often, and always feel a
certain moderation and dignity — serenity — given to me
in the reading." His familiarity with this author may
have led him to such thoughts as the following : —

" The Sphinx is a favorite symbol of mine — Nature —
who changes not but ever faces us with her problem. She
will utter no secret, but permits prying man to study
the inscriptions on her forehead, cheeks, and sides."

Both in writing and in conversation, Mr. Firth's remarkable quickness of wit, and strong faculty of comparison and analogy, caused him to introduce allusions
seemingly obscure, and to pass from one subject to another with a suddenness which would puzzle a slower
mind.

Of the intellectual companions whom he now had close
at hand and ready to answer his summons at a moment's
notice, no one, we think, gave him more frequent and
welcome counsel than Marcus Aurelius, whose philo-
sophical and analytical method of thought was so congenial to his own. Of this and of some other characteristics
we now take the opportunity to speak. With him, the
natural impulse was to find the " why" of action and emotion, and to arrive at the truth, the real interior meaning
of things. The following extracts, written only for his own
eye, will show this quality of mind.

" The man who travels around the world from west to
east, lives one more day, but no longer time ; nor does he
who loses a day by contrary travel, live a shorter time.
Suppose the swiftness of motion of the one increased in-
definitely, and that of the other to be as the motion of the

earth ; then, while the one lived an indefinite number of days, the other would live but one. The number of days in a man's life is no proper measure of its length. It is the curse of these conventions of time and space that a day is considered a day, whether long or short ; a month a month, though shorter than an hour. The truer measures are events. The time of the world is measured by celestial events, and the time of life should be, equally, by human. Are you young ; are you old? You may be, and you may not be ; nor can I tell one whit better by seeing your birth-note." Then follows a suggestion for drawing time-maps, whereon the distances of different places from any common centre should be regulated by the time required to travel those distances ; and after further examination into the nature of time and space, he ends thus : " Time without space cannot be imagined, nor the contrary. Time cannot have preceded matter, any more than matter can *outlive mind.*"

" It is surely good to be sometimes sick, — as necessary as mistakes are to confirm a man in his caution. The virtues of an active and a passive life seem to be quite different ; in place of courage, patience ; instead of resistance, submission ; yet the paradox holds, that we may conquer by yielding, and purchase victory in general, by defeats in particular."

" The same treatment which we accept graciously from one person, we will not tolerate from another, and I think the sympathy or equality between ourself and another is greater in the latter case. When the parties are quite unequal, one has no thought of redress, and this difference may be so great as to destroy the idea of retaliation. Would a

horse bear equally severe treatment from another horse?
[as from a man?] or a man accept from another man what
does not anger him when coming from the horse? We
feel offended in proportion as it is in our power to return
the affront, and when it is utterly beyond our power, then
there is no offence. If a man could punish a machine,
torture a locomotive, or burn fire, he would have other feelings when he suffered from them. An expression that I
should not regard, but that a friend has applied it to me,
stings. All this leads ultimately to the conclusion that
love and hate are only capable of existing between crea-
tures possessing similar faculties." He then continues the
same line of reasoning, to prove the personal nature of
God. "A man cannot love a stick (unless it simply
stand as representative of an imagined creature, having
powers like his own), nor hate fire, or water, or poison, or
a knife. If God were altogether different from man, we
could not love him."

The character of a mind must determine the nature of
its religious thought, and his intellect being such as it was,
he was often obliged, for truth's sake, to travel a long and
weary way about, in order to reach the goal, and understand what simpler minds are content to take for granted,
or to see by intuition. In theological discussions he rarely took any part when at home; but a dear friend of his at
Atchison, a gentleman of other opinions from his own, says
that they had several free conversations on the subject,
and that Mr. Firth always avowed his convictions to be
Unitarian. As no society of the same views existed in
Atchison, he had of late attended the Episcopal church.
While in Boston, he might have been seen occasionally at

the Catholic, and in the churches of the several Evangelical bodies, drawn there by the music, by a noted preacher, or by his own sense of fairness, which forbade his rejecting views, before he had heard them stated and defended by their upholders. He brought, in a word, the same openness and candor here, which he carried into his scientific studies.

But his practical religion was a daily, living fact. It touched him much more nearly than systems of belief or schemes of salvation. His purpose pointed to the highest, straight as a beam of light.

"You learned," he wrote to a friend, "how divine self-conquest, at the price of almost self-annihilation, is. You were wrong to call that overcoming the world; it is a rarer, nobler accomplishment, not at all conflicting with the maxims I quoted. The Stoic, having overcome the world, may hope to subject himself absolutely to duty and honor. Don't you see how unlike these supplementary parts of the hero are? for either lacking, he cannot follow principle to the death."

Mr. Firth was always something of a Stoic, especially in his younger days, when, as he has himself confessed, he found a certain attraction in doing a thing because it was hard for him to do it. Indeed, he was made of stern stuff; but, from the first, he turned the power of his strong will towards all good accomplishment, subjecting it, to use his own words, "to duty and honor." Nor was his strength hard and barren ; but, like a solid rock, it underlay a wealth of good deeds and human kindness.

Action was his easiest speech. His reserved and sensitive nature, and the difficulty of expressing his feelings, enhanced by their very intensity, made him seem stiff and cold, and formed a barrier between himself and others, even his nearest friends ; but that reserve once broken through, either from within or without, his few, short words concentrated the glow of many longer speeches. He could feel quickly the joys and sorrows of others though, like many another man with head full of plans, and heart in his work, he was almost unable at times to attend to anything else, and his letters seemed then to scarcely respond to those from home.

In boyhood he had not formed many close friendships, nor did he till much later add greatly to their number, though ready to offer courtesy and assistance wherever he could do so. He has been seen, when leaving the house of a friend at the same time with a little Irish girl whom he knew, to take from her her basket of cold food and carry it as far as their roads lay together.

When ill or exhausted, he did not escape those times of depression to which a nervous and high-strung temperament is liable; but returning strength, and hearty, satisfactory work, always restored the balance. He tried to meet all events with calmness. " I work here as conscientiously as in me lies," he wrote in 1871, " and am well contented that what is within my control goes well ; while Marcus Aurelius taught me long ago to be undisturbed by what happened over which I had no control. All I want to tell you is, that I think I have the secret of peace of mind ; it is to do your own part as fully and well as you can, and feel neither fear nor hope about the consequences."

Of things which he felt most deeply, he did not care to

speak much, and it was only from brief glimpses that those
who knew him best could guess his quiet depth of sentiment. He liked to remember anniversaries of happy days,
cherished little reminders of people whom he cared for,
and while living among strangers, far from home, he used
to carry the key of his father's house always in his pocket.
Yet even in writing, the expression of such feeling was
difficult to him, and many a sentence, begun full of emotion, he turned off with a joke.

He was ever ready to look up to what he felt above him,
and though critical and hard to please, had always his
heroes, whom he delighted to honor. To devote himself
to some person, some work, some idea, was his impulse ;
and his imagination was ever fired by any touch of such
devotion in books, or real life. To a loyal spirit like this,

> " To take
> So barren seems, when it can make
> Such bliss, for the beloved sake,
> Of bitter tasks."

His aim being so honest and so pure, he was ready,
when convinced he was wrong, to turn fairly about, confess
himself so, and alter his course, letting no false pride stand
in the way. " May I overcome the desire to manifest in-
dignation at ignorance. I have been very unreasonable
to-day, and am sorry," he wrote in his private journal.
Indeed, his metal was good steel, needing only life's gradual burnishing. It was controlled intensity,

> "A sword of fire, in a sheath of snow."

Judge Thacher, of Lawrence, wrote to Mr. Firth's
father, August 21, 1872 : " I met your son last June, at

Topeka, before the State Board of Assessors of railroad property. He there represented his road, and I distinctly remember the plain, pithy, and concise way that the details of his road were presented by him. No road had a more useful, careful, or influential representative, and, in addition to a carefully prepared statement of assets resources, and liabilities, he also made an oral, off-hand argument to show why the board should not make too high a valuation of his road. His reasoning was clear, convincing, and persuasive, and his road secured the lowest assessment of any, save one, I believe. He bade me good-by before the board closed, saying he must hurry back to Atchison to urge on his business."

His last time-table, No. 9, which was to take effect June 5th, 1872, at 4 A. M., shows a length of road of one hundred and twelve miles, with nineteen stations, the last being Sterling, Nebraska, and eight trains running daily. At the end of this table we find a new name, " M. M. Towne, Assistant Superintendent." Some time before, Mr. Firth had asked for a helper, as he was hard pressed with the largely-increased business of the road. He now wrote: " I shall be much more at liberty, freed from details which others can attend to equally well, with time to give to our general relations, and to cultivate our business, by which I can most effectually serve the road."

He had long ago promised to enter Lincoln July 4th, and now he seemed likely to be able to keep his word. On Thursday, June 6th, he wrote from the office on the boarding-train at the end of the track, one hundred and twenty-two miles from Atchison: " I see our large bridge party busy upon the fifteenth crossing of the Nemaha. . . .

We have twenty-four miles of iron yet to lay, and intend
to reach Lincoln July 1st. . . . While we are laying a
mile of track a day at the front, and with storm succeeding storm as they have done this season, you understand
that one or two persons must be on the *qui vive.*"

While he was writing, another storm was rising. Its
results were such that for the next two nights Mr. Firth
found no time for sleep. He was seen on the second
night (Friday), working with his men, knee-deep in mud,
taking hold wherever help was needed in getting upon the
track freight cars thrown off by the yielding of submerged
sleepers.

He made a little call in Atchison, Saturday morning,
and when he again started up the line, Mr. Allen accompanied him. They stopped to examine bridge No. 35,
which crossed a ravine. The central support was pronounced unsafe by Mr. Firth. Carpenters were set at
work, and instructed to stop trains and transfer passengers, and if their repairing was not finished at night, to be
on hand with lights.

The friends then went on beyond White Cloud, Mr.
Firth looking carefully over his track, bridges, cuts, and
embankments, for every record of the storm. They waited
at White Cloud, on their return, for the mail train for
Atchison, which arrived six hours late.

And now the week's work is done, the damages by
flood and accident repaired, and the weary superintendent
swings himself lightly upon the locomotive, saying all is
ready for Monday. He will sit upon the forward part,
with his feet resting on the pilot [or cow-catcher], that he
may again see his track and more quickly discern the ex-

pected signal of a coming freight train. Soon Mr. Allen joins him, as he "always goes where Firth is," and the two dear friends pass pleasant moments together, all unconscious that one is soon to meet his instant death, and the other to endure hours of torture. Of those happy moments we have no record, and can only rejoice in the true friendship which we know must have brightened the time as they sped on their homeward way.

In the mean time, the men left at the bridge had been busy at their task, and, as the night drew on, had completed it. Mr. Taylor, their foreman, says that new subsills had been put under some of the supports, and that every part of it had been carefully examined by himself, as well as by his men, and pronounced safe by all. A freight train of twelve cars, some of which were loaded, was then waiting on the north side of the ravine for the signal to cross. Attached to it was the heaviest locomotive in the service, weighing thirty-two tons.

On a previous page, Mr. Firth has described the emotions of men in charge of such a bridge when a locomotive and cars first go over it, and the same anxiety is felt when it is first tried after repairs.

Mr. Taylor took the best place for critical observation while the train went upon and over the bridge, and at the same time placed his men in other positions where they could together have a view of it in every part.

It stood this crucial test.

Not only did the train pass safely, but no perceptible deflection in the bridge was seen by any of these experienced observers. That Mr. Taylor had a right, after that, to consider the bridge safe, and to send word to his Superintendent, "There is no longer danger here," will not be questioned by the men of his calling. And word did reach Mr. Firth, on his way down, of the passage of this train.

Mr. Taylor remembered, he says, how thorough and how cautious his chief was ; he "never knew an engineer take such pains where risks of life were involved" ; confirming the words of another trusted employee, that Mr. Firth "had not a man who would not go anywhere he directed, because each knew he was not the sort to run unnecessary risks, or to send a man where he would not go himself."

Mr. Taylor again examined the foundations, including that upon the shoulder of the ravine on the north side. "If," he says, "it had yielded, or if any danger lurked there, it was hidden from human sight." [For a description of this bridge, and a statement of the causes of its fall, see Appendix.]

Signals to warn approaching trains were no longer necessary. The dangers and labors of that trying week were over. So it seemed to these men, and they left for their several homes, more than ready for that blessed rest between Saturday night and Monday morning, which the faithful laborer only can fully know.

The removal of this last obstruction from his road was reason enough for the buoyant cheerfulness of the Superintendent, of which we have spoken. "I never saw him when he felt better," said one. "The Major had had as hard a time as anybody," said another, "but nobody had been hurt. Nothing worse than a few hours' detention had happened to any train, and we all hoped and believed that the great rains which had come right after one another for a month, were over, as we had never known so many of them before."

The conductor of this train was Mr. F. G. Rice. He had been told by Mr. Firth, when he first met him that day, that bridge No 35 was unsafe, and Mr. Rice had instructed his engineman to stop just before reaching it. The information subsequently received by Mr. Firth of its having been crossed by the freight train, was not known to Mr. Rice. The reason may have been that safety did not require the conductor to know this, and that, from their respective places on the train, neither could see the other without inconvenience and delay.

It was about nine o'clock when the train approached the bridge. A whistle to apply the brakes was sounded and the speed slackened to four or five miles per hour. Mr. Firth then signalled the engineman to " go ahead." The locomotive had not gone upon the bridge more than fifteen feet, when it plunged to the bottom of the ravine !

The tender followed, resting upon the rear end of the locomotive, while the cars of the train remained in safety upon the track, just north of what had now become a chasm.

On its way down, the pilot either came in contact with the rails of the falling bridge, or with that part of the bridge yet standing (probably the former), and was thrust over upon the locomotive where the two young men were seated..

It was this that instantly killed the younger.

It was a part of this, which, missing his body, caught the right arm of the elder between itself and the front of the locomotive, known as the saddle, and held the arm as in a vise. He was almost buried, at the same moment, in the nauseous mud and water of the bottom, and cut off from immediate help by the débris from the pilot and bridge timbers. His arm, unhappily, was behind him when it was struck by the pilot, and this enforced position, from which escape, unaided, was impossible, brought the upper part of his body against the hot front of the smoke-arch to be burned ; but his immediate danger was suffocation.

Conductor Rice was the first to descend into the ravine, and to know that which has forever saddened many hearts.

So sudden had been the fall, that neither the engineman (Mr. Strahan) nor the fireman (Mr. Drummond) had time to escape. They were first thrown forward against the boiler. They then sprang for the windows of the cab, and thence jumped to the ground, a distance of ten or twelve feet. Fortunately both escaped with only bruises which did not prevent their rendering effective service afterward.

It was three A. M. of Sunday, the 9th of June, before Mr. Firth was released. Of that time, during which the minutes must have stretched to hours and the hours to eternities, the sufferer never spoke afterwards, except in the most general terms. All, however, who were with him bear testimony to his wonderful heroism ; to his self-control ; to his clear comprehension of what was necessary to be done and how best to do it ; and to his thorough appreciation of the untiring efforts of his men to free him from his awful situation.

On the one hand, he saw that a want of caution might cause the locomotive to settle further and crush him ; while on the other, no time should be lost because of his suffer-

8

ings, and also because one of the sudden rises of the creek might occur and drown him.

But his ever-recurring thought was for his companion. "Where is Allen?" "Is Allen safe?" "Why don't Allen come?" were his inquiries. Evasive answers were given, such as, that Allen was "doing well." They feared the effect, should they say, "He is dead."

The body of his friend was easily extricated and reverently cared for; and it was not till the next day, at Atchison, that in answer to his startling question, "Is Allen dead?" the truth was confessed.

Mr. Drummond, the fireman, says that when he reached Mr. Firth, he found him "doubled up under the smoke-arch, his feet up, and his body in the mud and water." It was Mr. Drummond who removed the mud from his face, thus enabling him to breathe freely, and liberated his left arm. He asked for "water, water." Brandy was found and given him. He said, "Help me, help me." On being assured that everything possible would be done for him, he said, "I believe you."

"He gave directions to his men," said one of the passengers in the train, "as if his final release were only a question of time, and his life were not imperilled." When told of the progress that was made, he would say, "That's good! encourage me." Feeling his head with his left hand, he said, "My head is cut; but it is all right, if you can get my arm out." At another time he said: "My arm pains me dreadfully. I believe it is broken; but don't cut it." He thought if the engine could be jacked up two or three inches, he could pull his arm out. Stretching out his hand, he said, "Jones, take hold," and made many attempts to free himself. Once he said, " Don't think I am frightened. I have not had any sleep for forty-eight hours, and am only nervous."

It was necessary to secure the locomotive where it was, and it required time and caution to find and adjust, in the dark, the ropes and timbers necessary. Two men at most, and during the greater part of the time one only, could work directly in removing the part of the pilot which held him ; so contracted was the available space, and so great the care that was thought necessary. It is enough, that all did their best.

In spite of his indomitable will, Mr. Firth's mind wandered at times, as the night wore on; but such reliefs were not of long duration.

Two expressions of a more general nature than any we have given, have been attributed to him. One was, " I 'm crushed by an engine. Tell my friends how I came to my death, doing my duty to my country and my railroad company." This sentiment was in harmony with all his life, for duty was the master thought of his being.

The other expression was : " Jesus, save me, save me !" We know not if the words that came to his lips were spoken in full consciousness or not ; but in that night of agony we cannot doubt that angels ministered to him, and that around him were the " everlasting arms " of the Father, whom with reverent, intelligent thought he earnestly sought to know, and in whose service his life of faithful, useful goodness was lived.

Surgical aid was sent for from White Cloud and Atchison. Drs. Cochrane and Burge of the latter place arrived about the time of Mr. Firth's deliverance. Accompanying them was Mr. M. M. Towne, the Assistant Superintendent. It would be a pleasant duty to record the names of all who remained with him on this night, working for his relief or assuaging his sufferings, and of those who went for help of any kind from near or far. This we can hardly hope to do. We can only give such as have been made known to us. They are Messrs. F. Taylor, J. C. Moore, and A. P. Jones ; Conductors Rice, Graves and Filson ; Fireman Drummond ; Engineman Strahan, and Trainman Finnegan ; Mr. Firth's young friend, Mr. J. W. Lincoln, and, later, Messrs. Clark and Bostwick.

The last blow for his deliverance was at length given. Piece by piece the obdurate wood and iron had yielded, and the form which six hours before was instinct with an amazing force in every part, was brought out of that miry pit, mutilated and prostrate. It had escaped death as if by miracle ; it had endured shocks and agonies which would have proved mortal to one less hardened by labor and training, or less youthful.

Thankfulness was in every heart. So great was the faith in his vitality and victorious will, that it was the general belief he would surely survive. It was said : "They could not kill him." "Nobody else would have lived through it." "We expected he would hold out because he said he should."

He was wrapped in a blanket and carried to the house of a neighboring farmer, Mr. Flick, where he was attended by the surgeons. Everything possible was done for him by Mr. Flick and his family. Chloroform was given him, and then, at peace after such a heart-rending struggle, he

was taken in the train to Atchison, where he arrived about
five o'clock in the morning.   What a contrast to the expected return there at ten o'clock the night before! Ah,
if God ever gave to man the choice between immediate
death and life on such conditions, the answer must be,
" No, no, not life ! "

Soon Dr. J. H. Stringfellow came to give his young
friend his most skilful, tender, and unremitting services.

It was found' necessary to amputate Mr. Firth's right
arm above the elbow.   His head had a cut about five
inches long, over the left parietal bone ; there were deep
and broad burns upon his back, shoulders, neck, and arms ;
bruises in various parts of his body, and, underlying all,
the want of sleep, and the prostration of his nervous system.
The practised eyes of his surgeons pronounced the case
very critical, and rest was the one indispensable condition.

The appalling news had gone through the town like the
lightning's flash.   There was not a heart unmoved.   Men
and women, by a common impulse, thronged to his cham-
ber with their offers of personal service, and also of whatever their houses contained.   In the several churches,
prayers for his recovery were offered.

It was the mourning of a city.   One of its chiefs, and
the youngest of all, had fallen with his armor on, while
extending and perfecting one of the works on which its
hopes of the future rested.   Indeed, a personal interest in
such improvements runs through Western communities,
and naturally attaches, also, to the men who direct them.
If such men were chosen by the citizens, with a direct
responsibility to them, the relation would hardly be closer.

Because of this, and also because of the work he had

already done; because of his character, his youth, his heroism, his sufferings, and the startling nature of the event, which had at the same time removed from their midst another young man, less known, but of the highest promise, — all that was generous and tender in a people deficient in neither quality, instantly and universally responded.

Upon Mr. Towne rested the duty of making the event known to the friends at Boston. About nine A. M. he sent the following message.

ATCHISON, KANSAS, June 9th, 1872.

A. FIRTH : —

Engine fell through bridge last night. O. E. Allen killed ; your son seriously injured. Right arm amputated, and he is cut about the head. Doctors consider him in a very critical condition. Will telegraph daily. One of our men will start to-day or to-morrow, with the remains of Allen. Notify his mother.

M. M. TOWNE,
Ass't Supt.

The bright Sunday noon brought this terrible message to Mr. Firth's home.

The first care was for the widowed mother who had lost her only son. When arrangements had been made for sending to her the dreadful tidings, the next work was for Mr. Firth's father to arrange pressing business matters, so as to leave on Monday for Atchison. In the mean while the blessed telegraph kept the family informed of the sufferer's condition, and gave them hope of reaching him while living. Also, to their great comfort, came word at midnight that Mr. Kendall, of Leavenworth, skilled in the care of the sick (whose kindness and interest in Mr. Firth had been shown at the time of his illness at Lawrence), was with him, and would remain until they arrived. Indeed, he did more than that, — bringing from Leavenworth a known and trusted surgeon, Dr. Weaver, to add his skill to that already employed. Nor did Mr. Kendall's own wise and welcome care cease until there was no more need for earthly watching.

Monday saw Mr. and Mrs. Firth and daughter on their anxious journey, cheered by the kind offices of friends who did all that could be done to speed them on their way, or encourage them with messages from the sick-room. The cordial and efficient sympathy of the railway officials can never be forgotten by that sad company. At Chicago, friends welcomed them, and after a few moments for refreshment, they were rushing over the prairies in a special train, to Quincy, provided by the generous liberality of Mr. Robert Harris, of the Chicago, Burlington and Quincy Railroad. From Quincy to St. Joseph, the same marked courtesy was extended to them by Mr. G. H. Nettleton, of the Hannibal and St. Joseph, and from St. Joseph to Winthrop, by Mr. D. H. Winton, of the Kansas City, St. Joseph and Council Bluffs railways, the distances on the three roads exceeding five hundred miles.

Sixty hours from Boston brought the travellers to Atchison, and, in the early dawn of Thursday, they stood by the sick-bed, warmly welcomed by their precious invalid. With justifiable pride, he enjoyed the high compliment implied in the giving of an extra train, " partly to father, and partly to me," he said ; "and now I am glad father will

have an opportunity to know something of these generous
Western railway men whom I value so highly."

With all the welcome a sick man could give, he showed
his joy in their coming, having his room decorated with
forest boughs, and calling attention to the flowers friends
had sent him.

Through nearly one week of alternate hope and fear on
the part of relatives and friends, his life trembled in the
balance.   But the hurts were all too great for healing.
The skilful care of attentive surgeons, the loving service
of friends, could not save his precious life.

On Wednesday, June 19th, the spirit left the shattered
body, to pass unfettered on its upward way.

The lucid intervals of that sickness have left treasured
memories ; of tender thought of the dead companion whom
he mourned far beyond his own losses and sufferings ; of
a brave spirit, looking unflinchingly at his own life with
his right arm gone forever ; of thought of friends both
near and far.   For the most part, however, the uncon-
sciousness which saved him fearful suffering from his
dreadful wounds, veiled the noble spirit seen only in occa-
sional glimpses, as the blue of heaven between the clouds
of earth.

But we should fail utterly in speaking of that sick-room,
did we not attempt some slight tribute to the constant,
thoughtful kindness, which, within and without that cham-
ber, ministered both to the sick youth and his anxious
family.   Words cannot express it, but in the soil of grateful hearts it lies, we trust maturing for new service when
others' needs shall call ; the only way in which such **disin**-
terested gifts can be fitly repaid.

On a lovely June evening the still form was carried to the Episcopal church which he had attended, and, after service there, was laid at rest in a beautiful rural cemetery, just as the last rays of the setting sun fell upon the knoll where the new grave was made. Nor was it altogether painful to leave the dear, lifeless body in that land where he had done his manhood's work, and where he had won for himself hosts of true friends, who will long keep for him a place of love in their hearts, and honor in their memories.

There remains for them, and for all to whom the knowledge may come, an example of honor, fidelity, integrity, thoughtfulness for others, industry, large practical and scholarly attainments, and brilliant success in his chosen calling.

Conspicuously he had the dearest love of all who were near him, the highest respect of his widely-scattered acquaintances, and the rarest devotion of the men who served under him.

To his friends at home he has left memories of a pure boyhood and the opening of a splendid manhood.

For the sake of others, such a life seemed to merit, nay, to demand this record, however inadequate it may be ; but let no one infer that the life was perfect. While it calls for no defence, such a claim has not been thought of.

In its own simplicity we leave it, inexpressibly thankful to Him who gave it, for all that it was.

But our eyes will glance to the future which awaited him here, and which shone so brightly when the summons to depart came. O, the loss! the loss! we find ourselves repeating ; loss to his friends ; to his profession ; to the community in which he moved ; and to his country. Where is the compensation ? Alas ! we know not. It must suffice that he was in the line of his duty, and that results are with God.

We speak lightly, often, of the engineer's work as only one means of gaining a livelihood. " Every road leads to the end of the world," so every work faithfully done, and every life nobly lived, lead to the highest goal. But the opening of a new country to the opportunities of civilization, the building of bridges and roads on which coming generations shall pass to life and duty in new regions, are works fraught with illimitable consequences and opportunities which must move any thoughtful mind engaged in such a service. Such considerations add nobility to the mechanical work of this calling, and must give deeper content in a career pursued often under great trials and disabilities.

We cannot think of this young life as finished, but rather with its broad foundations grandly laid, like some proud monument whose firm base is founded wide and deep on earth, but whose perfected shaft stretches up beyond our sight to catch the rays of light as they spring unclouded from their living source.

APPENDIX.

MR. O. E. ALLEN.

HYMN

Sung at the burial of Otis Everett Allen, who died in the discharge of his duty on the railroad near Atchison, Kansas, June 8, 1872, at the age of twenty-two : —

(Auld Lang Syne.)

"The sweet June day is almost done ;
   The shadows, lengthening, fall ;
And tenderly the setting sun
   Shines in on bier and pall.
And shadows gather on the heart,
   And eyes with tears are dim,
While sadly now, before we part,
   We sing his funeral hymn.

"No more, in thronging college halls,
   Our brother's face is seen ;
No more that vigorous footstep falls
   On pleasant college green.
The voice is still, and cold the hand,
   The strong, free life is fled ;
And kindred, classmates, friends, **we stand**
   In presence of the dead.

"The work is done he did so well ;
   Closed is the swift career ;
At duty's chosen post he fell,
   Without a pain or fear.

Amid the forms he loved the best,
Beneath the springing sod,
We lay the broken form to rest, —
The life is hid with God.

NORTHBOROUGH, June 12, 1872.

Extract from a letter written by Mrs. Allen : —

"When Everett (Mr. Allen) left me, he dropped off his boyhood and clothed himself in the dignity of the true, manly nature which was his rightful inheritance. He went, determined to win his way to a position which would make his mother proud of him, — as though I had not always been proud of the bright, beautiful, courteous boy, who believed in his mother as few boys do, and who never lost his baby purity in the contact with other boys, or his high sense of honor, or integrity of purpose. And when he found in your son a young man of like spirit, just enough older to be a guide and yet not too old for constant companionship, he felt that his cup was very full, and his chances of success very great. . . . I felt that —— would have a right to blame me, if the boy failed of a splendid and noble manhood. And in this comes the only ray of light. He did not fail ; and though he had no time to really show himself, yet he had time to convince us all that *we*, his home friends, were not mistaken in him. . . . Of course, we know they are together, and if we have no reason for this faith, let us hold to it ; else where were our heaven ? What would it be without those nearest and dearest to us ? . . . God help us to live such lives as shall fit us to walk with them when we come into the light of that wonderful life beyond the grave."

THE BRIDGE;

WITH REMARKS AS TO THE POSITION OF THE YOUNG MEN, AND SOME INCIDENTS OMITTED IN THE NARRATIVE.

THE bridge, which must now be long associated with the names of Firth and Allen, was one and a half miles north of Highland Station, and was of the usual trestle kind. In that soil, almost free from rocks, the streams have been able to open for themselves, at frequent intervals, such channels of variable depth and width, as can only be crossed by bridges. This was the thirty-fifth in a distance of only twenty-seven miles from Atchison. It was about ninety-six feet long and eighteen feet high. It was supported by four rows of upright posts, each post twelve by twelve inches, and each row resting upon four large sub-sills imbedded in the earth. On the north side of the ravine, *i. e.* the side towards White Cloud, there was a shoulder of eight or ten feet in width about half-way down the bank. The posts nearest to that side rested upon this shoulder.

The bridge was not built by Mr. Firth, but was among the structures in use when that part of the road came into the possession of the Atchison and Nebraska Railroad Company. It had been repaired as occasion required. Its timbers were sound, and it was considered, both by Mr. Firth and by his foreman who had charge of it, as safe as any on the road. One of its supports had been affected by the floods, which had nearly filled the ravine during the latter part of May and the beginning of June. It was this fact which arrested the attention of Mr. Firth as he went up the line on the 8th of June, and made necessary the work upon it that day.

The new sub-sills were nine to ten feet long, twelve inches thick, and from eighteen to twenty inches wide. Mr. Taylor says his orders were " to remain at the bridge until it was safe."

An examination into the immediate cause of its fall subsequently showed it to have been a settling of the sub-sills in the shoulder. These were found to have penetrated into a quicksand. This shoulder had been under water several days before ; but at the time of which we are speaking, the water in the channel was less than three feet deep. Of course, while under water, the earth, or outer shell of the quicksand, was softened ; and each train must have forced the sills a little deeper, until they rested only upon the treacherous sand. This was the hidden danger spoken of by Mr. Taylor, over which, however, trains had passed and repassed in safety for several years, and which he had not been able to detect in two careful examinations of the spot on that afternoon.

If ever there was an accident of which it could be truthfully stated that none concerned in it were to blame, this was one. Not only was there no want of ordinary caution on the part of Mr. Taylor and his men ; but, as the narrative has shown, they were more than usually observant ; and if no other evidence existed, the safe passage of the freight train is his and their vindication.

That passage, as has been already stated, was known to the superintendent. He knew also, from experience, the competency of the foreman he had left at the bridge. When Mr. Taylor said it was safe, and could point to such a confirmation of his judgment, there was no longer room for mistrust. It would not then have been caution, but timidity, which would have led the most careful manager to hesitate about sending his trains over it.

The painful reflection is, that the risk was not special, but general, and attaches to all such structures in such a soil.

We have seen how disturbed the track of the Atchison and Nebraska had been by floods. To Mr. Firth, who knew every inch of his road, it was most natural and proper, nay inevitable, that he should improve every opportunity for observation. Hence, the habit of sitting in front of the boiler of the locomotive. And besides this general reason, on that night there was the special one stated in the narrative.

But death and injury came from an incident of which no previous experience could have given warning to the young men. This was the doubling of the pilot upon them. Had the timbers of the bridge broken, or had the whole structure fallen, either of which accidents was far more likely to occur than that a support in the rear should sink under them, the pilot would have kept its proper position and gone first into the mud of the bottom. In that event, the young men, both of singular activity, would have been free, and all the probabilities against a fatal result.

Had Mr. Firth and his friend been in a passenger car, as we now see, they would have escaped; but with the light which Mr. Firth then had, and his high sense of personal responsibility for the condition of his road and the safety of his trains, that was not the place for him. It is, alas! possible that his standard of fidelity was too high; but fatal as its results have been to us and ours, we leave to others the inculcation of a lower one.

THE FUNERAL OF MR. FIRTH.

Rev. P. N. Meade, the rector of Trinity Church, read the service and preached a sermon from the 40th chapter of Isaiah, 7th and 8th verses. The choir sang "The Silent Land," "Let me know my end," and, by request of the family, Montgomery's hymn, beginning, —

> " Go to the grave in all thy glorious prime,
>   In full activity of zeal and power," —

closing, at the church, with the hymn Mr. Firth had heard there on a previous Sunday, the pleasure derived from which he had at the time expressed to members of the choir : —

> " Softly now the light of day
>   Fades upon my sight away."

At the grave, in Mount Vernon cemetery, appropriate selections were also sung.

Grateful acknowledgments are due to the rector and to each one of the choir, for their tender and heartfelt tributes.

CORRESPONDENCE IN REGARD TO A MONUMENT.

Atchison, Kansas.

Abraham Firth, Esq. :

Respected Sir, — On behalf of the employees of the Atchison and Nebraska Road, we have the honor to enclose a draft for $911.25, subscribed by them for the erection of a monument in the memory of your son, our late superintendent and chief engineer, F. R. Firth.

This testimonial is the spontaneous tribute of men who, associated with him in daily work, honored and loved him, and who desire, in some material way, to testify the high esteem and respect in which they held him.

His devotion to duty, his untiring energy, and his sterling integrity of character endeared him alike to all employees of the company, to the people of the country traversed by the road he so ably and successfully managed, and to all he came into contact with. His work was his life, and he brought to it a clear and vigorous intellect, a mind remarkably well stored with information, organizing and executive ability of the highest character, and an industry and energy that never seemed to weary or want rest. Young as he was, the high place he held made him neither arrogant nor vain. He required at all times, of his employees, a strict performance of their duties ; but he was ever courteous, kind, and just.

He met with his death in the discharge of his duty. He bore, with unshrinking fortitude and courage, the dreadful pain of that night of agony and terror, and the long suffering that finally terminated in his death.

Remembering with affection his noble manhood and sterling worth, and mourning sincerely his untimely death, we desire to assure you, and all of his surviving relatives, of our deep sympathy with you in your affliction, and of our high regard and esteem for your son. And we therefore ask you to receive and appropriate to the erection of a monument to his memory the money herewith sent.

COMMITTEE,

For the Employees of the A. and N. Railroad Company.

BOSTON, MASS., October 14th, 1872.

To the Subscribers to the Fund for the Monument to F. R. Firth:

The committee to whom you entrusted your subscription for the above purpose, sent me, promptly, its sum; being nine hundred and eleven dollars and twenty-five cents ($911.25), with an able and welcome letter.

Upon the subscription papers are 364 names, all, as I understand, employees of the Atchison and Nebraska Railroad. Having then been in my son's service, and so held personal relations with him, this testimony has an added, and a priceless value.

In my own name, and in the name of each member of my family, I would profoundly thank you, one and all.

And while this tribute is in the highest degree honorable to your late superintendent, it is no less so to you. This appreciation of his worth, and this manifestation of it by his fellow-laborers, will arrest the attention and command the reverence of the generous and thoughtful wherever it shall be known.

You send me the gift without conditions as to where the monument shall be erected; but you evidently expected it would be in his native State. It was the original purpose of his family to have removed his body here in due time; but the unbounded love and honor shown his memory by the people of Atchison had led us to hesitate, and now your grand act has reversed our first decision.

Both his grave and monument will be at Atchison, where his work as a man was chiefly done.

With unspeakable gratitude, I am very truly and cordially your friend,

ABRAHAM FIRTH.

TRIBUTES.

THE following are among the resolutions passed at a meeting of the officers and employees of the Atchison and Nebraska Railroad, held June 20, 1872 : —

Resolved, That in the death of our superintendent, we are called upon to mourn the loss of a bright ornament to his profession, a faithful, energetic, and conscientious officer, a firm and unwavering friend to the interests of our city and our road, and, above all, a friend and counsellor to whom we could at all times look with profound respect.

" *Resolved,* That during our connection with this road, nothing, from the first, has ever occurred to mar the harmony existing between us and our late superintendent; but that our intercourse has daily strengthened the warm friendship and profound respect with which we have ever regarded him.

" *Resolved,* That we tender our heartfelt sympathy to the bereaved family in their deep affliction, and, while we feel that all words are powerless, we point to the brief but brilliant career of our associate, as affording the best consolation to his afflicted relatives and friends.

" *Resolved,* That in respect to his memory, we will attend the funeral this afternoon in a body, and that we will wear the usual badge of mourning for thirty days."

From Mr. O. Chanute.

" I think I may say that I have never, during an experience of now some twenty-four years on public works, met a man of his age of greater promise, nor more happily fitted for the business of life, by nature and by education. He possessed the gift, now rare, of character, and united to a constant desire for knowledge the power of organizing and governing men.

" Living in an age of material development, he threw all his energies into that work. Seeing half a continent yet to subdue, he devoted himself to the management of the most powerful engine that has yet been tried for that purpose. In other ages, he might have been a scholar, or a priest, or a statesman ; in the nineteenth century, and in the United States, he aspired to excel as a railroad man. Had he lived, he would undoubtedly have rendered the country signal services, and been rewarded with fame and fortune; and yet it is unfortunate for all at the present day, that noble aims are so limited, and the rewards of such a material nature.

. . . " In fact, I think he was one of the best engineers of his age in the country, uniting with a sound judgment, thorough scientific attainments and a rare executive ability. Everything he did was well done, as well as judiciously and economically done.

" In addition to this, he had a firm and noble character, a high sense of justice, and an exacting standard of integrity."

" Major F. R. Firth died at five o'clock last evening, from the effects of the injuries he received on the 8th inst. "

" Rarely have we been called upon to publish intelligence that has been read with more sincere sorrow throughout all this region of country, than will be the brief paragraph above printed.

" During his brief residence in our city, Major Firth won and steadily held the confidence, respect, and genuine esteem of this entire community, as well as of the people of all the country traversed by the Atchison and Nebraska road. His reputation, too, had extended far and wide, and especially throughout all Kansas, Nebraska, and Western Missouri, he was regarded as one of the most able, energetic, and intelligent young railroad managers in the country. . . . He was but twenty-five years old, full of health, energy, and vital power, and as pure in heart as he was sound in body and strong and clear in brain.

" We made Major Firth's acquaintance shortly after his arrival in this city, and early conceived for him a high and sincere respect and esteem. We have rarely known a man so young as he, who was so well and so generally informed, who had as clear and vigorous an intellect, or who was endowed with so much energy, industry, and organizing and executive capacity. Nor have we ever known one who bore a sudden elevation to a position of high responsibility and great power with more becoming modesty and manly self-possession. It made him neither arrogant nor vain. He went about his new duties with a patient industry, an indomitable energy, a painstaking carefulness and zeal, and an inflexible integrity that were inherent in him, and that no circumstances or position in which he was placed could ever affect or destroy. His habits were as correct and his life as manly and pure as his energy and integrity were undoubted. A strong, noble manhood in him fittingly supplemented high capacities and the faithfulest devotion to duty.

" We heard of the dreadful accident that has put an end to his young and promising life, just as we were leaving New York for Boston, on Monday, a week ago, and rarely have we been so shocked and grieved. We have hoped against hope, ever since that time, that he might be spared. We record his death with unfeigned sorrow, and pen this tribute to his brief but brilliant career, and his manly and modest worth, with respectful and affectionate remembrance."

From the " Chicago Railway Review."

" Mr. Firth gained, with a rapidity very rare, the highest practical skill from experience, — a result due to an aptitude for practical engineering worthy to be called genius, seconded by a knowledge of the sciene that was singularly varied and profound. His, too, was a wonderful enthusiasm and an exhaustless energy, rendering easy the yoke and light the burdens of labor and responsibility in every department of railway engineering, construction, and operation. He took a high and manly pride in achievements certainly rare in one so young ; in the rapidly-expanding road he sought to realize his *beau ideal ;* and step by step, as it advanced through a country rich in resources but comparatively unpeopled, he, with fine spirit and sagacity, marked out policies of operating management, looking to rapid settlement and development. His nobility of nature, and energy and skill in his profession, were supplemented with personal qualities the most winning. His every word and act inspired respect ; his word was truth with the public, as well as law with those associated with him in management and work. Amid the ceaseless and complicated routine of construction and operation, he found time to retain mastership of his science, and especially to keep read up in the engineering literature of the day.

"While deploring the loss to his profession, and to the public interested in legitimate railway construction and prudent management, we may also be permitted to tender our heartfelt sympathies to the family bereft of the only son and brother in whom centred love so deep, so just a pride, and so fond an expectation."

Mr. J. F. Joy, his chief, under date of January 13, 1872, wrote to Mr. Firth : —

"I have your letter in relation to the offer" (referring to a proposition just made by the president of another railroad). "We shall much regret to lose you upon our road. . . . We do not wish to stand in your way, but rather to congratulate you on the better position and prospects offered and before you, — though they are simply what are due to your merits and ability."

As an illustration of Mr. Firth's spirit and self-respect, we cannot forbear quoting, in this connection, from a letter of his to an officer of the road to which it refers, dated January 28th, 1872 : —

"I am no seeker for office, am satisfied here, and have the confidence and approval of my employers. If I enter your service, it will be not as any man's friend or nominee, but as an engineer and railway man, ready to devote what energy and capacity I have, wholly to your service. . . . If I doubted my ability to perform the duties thoroughly and honestly, I should refuse to consider any offer. I do not say that I should not be glad to assume greater responsibilities than I have, but I wish to receive no favor or support on personal grounds."

NEW TOWN OF FIRTH.

"A SHORT distance from Lincoln is the town of Firth, which has been just laid out. It is named in honor of the memory of the late lamented superintendent of the road."
—*Western Paper, Sept.* 1872.

Firth is in the county of Lancaster and state of Nebraska. Its railway station is 125 miles north of Atchison, 21 miles south of Lincoln, and between Sterling and Hickman on the A. & N. R. R.

Extracts from letters written by men in Mr. Firth's employ.

"It was never in his power until after he sent for me to come here, to show to me how truly noble he was, and I shall always look back to this seemingly short year as the brightest and happiest of my life, and to the day that parted us as the saddest."

" He was a kind and generous friend to me. I never can forget him or his many acts of kindness to me."

" He was my best friend."

" When he lived I had a friend ; but now I have no friend to look to like him."

" He was the best friend I ever had. I always tried to do my duty and be a credit to him. I don't think I ever gave him any cause to regret the interest he had in my welfare. Although doing a great deal for me, he never hesitated to reprimand me if I did wrong. For the four years I was acquainted with him, I never knew him to do anything beneath the dignity or honor of a gentleman."

" He discharged his every duty without fear, and re-warded each employee as his own merits deserved."

" I shall always refer with pride to the many evidences of his approval in my possession, and to his often repeated thanks, which, with him, meant all that his language expressed."

" It was a pleasure to make a thing look good and stout, and straight and true, when Mr. Firth was here, as he always saw everything, and a smile from him was good pay for a hard day's work."

Extracts from private letters of friends.

" We express the deep sympathy of our hearts in the great and irreparable loss of your son, in the full bloom of early manhood, just as he had entered the front rank of his chosen and honorable profession, for which his gentlemanly deportment, abilities of a high order, and great force of character so well fitted him."

Signed by all the Superintendents of Railways in Boston.

"He had, in his boy-manhood, accomplished far more than the average of men credited with more than ordinary ability, in a long life, and his example and wonderful success will have great influence. His rare talent, his bravery and perseverance, won extreme admiration ; but my heart went out to him as it never did to another, save the nearest of kindred."

"His real life is untouched." It was "more noble in its aspirations, it seems to me, than that of any young man of his age I ever knew." "Excelsior" was "his motto in small as well as in great things."

"It is something to think what a brave, heroic life Frank's was, and how many years were condensed into those few. . . . May all the brave, good deeds of his life come, like holy angels, to comfort you. . . . I can never recall Frank but as living. He seems to me just approaching the house, just holding out his hand with that pleasant, shy smile of greeting."

"Sad as it is to give him up, it seems sadder still to think of what life might have been after such an experi-

ence of danger, suffering, and loss, and I would rather
think of him, as I do, as entering at once upon those new
duties and that higher life which we feel must be the position of such an active and faithful spirit."

"The loss so suddenly of our best and bravest and
dearest, is a wound that goes deep and lasts long. There
is no real comfort for such sorrows, except in the hardest
daily work and the highest spiritual trust, and the gradual
passing of the days and months and years. God does not
mean us to be comforted too soon. Sorrow has a tender
and invisible work to do in every one of us, and He takes
care that it shall be done to the uttermost, and as we
grow wise with time and thought, we learn to be thankful
for it. How, indeed, can we be anything but thankful for
every gift from the hand of Him who can only bless!
"A soul so good and noble as your boy will never be
lost out of the universe. He labored here for the common good, and now he has left his engines and his railway
works for some still higher calling."

"Human care and foresight could have done no more
than was done. The very act of going upon the forward
part of the engine, which made the fall fatal to your son
and his dear friend, was an act of extreme care and caution.
Is not such self-forgetful sacrifice akin to His who 'saved
others, but could not save Himself'? I like to feel the
kinship of such sacrifice with the free-will offering of the
cross, and learn from the mighty Sufferer how to bear the
cross that is laid upon us."

"Frank is safe. No temptations can reach him. No disastrous change can come within his circle. He drinks of the living river. He sings the new song."

SELECTIONS.

"Where is the hardship, then, if no tyrant, nor yet an unjust judge, sends thee away from the State, but nature who brought thee into it? the same as if a proctor who had employed an actor, dismisses him from the stage.

"'But I have not finished the five acts, but only three of them!'

"Thou sayest well, but in life the three acts are the whole drama; for what shall be a complete drama is determined by Him who was once the cause of its composition, and now of its dissolution; but thou art the cause of neither. Depart then, satisfied, for He, also, who releases thee is satisfied."

Marcus Aurelius.

"Show those qualities, then, which are altogether in thy power; sincerity, gravity, endurance of labor, aversion to pleasure, contentment with thy position and with few things, frankness, no love of superfluity, freedom from trifling, magnanimity.'

Ditto.

" My love involves the love before ;
   My love is vaster passion now ;
   Though mixed with God and nature thou,
I seem to love thee more and more.

" Far off thou art, but ever nigh ;
   I have thee still, and I rejoice.
   I prosper, circled by thy voice ;
   I shall not lose thee though I die !

" In Memoriam.

" Be thou faithful unto death, and I will give thee a crown of life."

Rev. ii. 10.

" Wherefore let them that suffer according to the will of God, commit the keeping of their souls to Him in well doing, as unto a faithful Creator."

1st Peter iv. 19.

" For God created man to be immortal, and made him to be an image of his own eternity."

Wisdom of Solomon ii. 23.

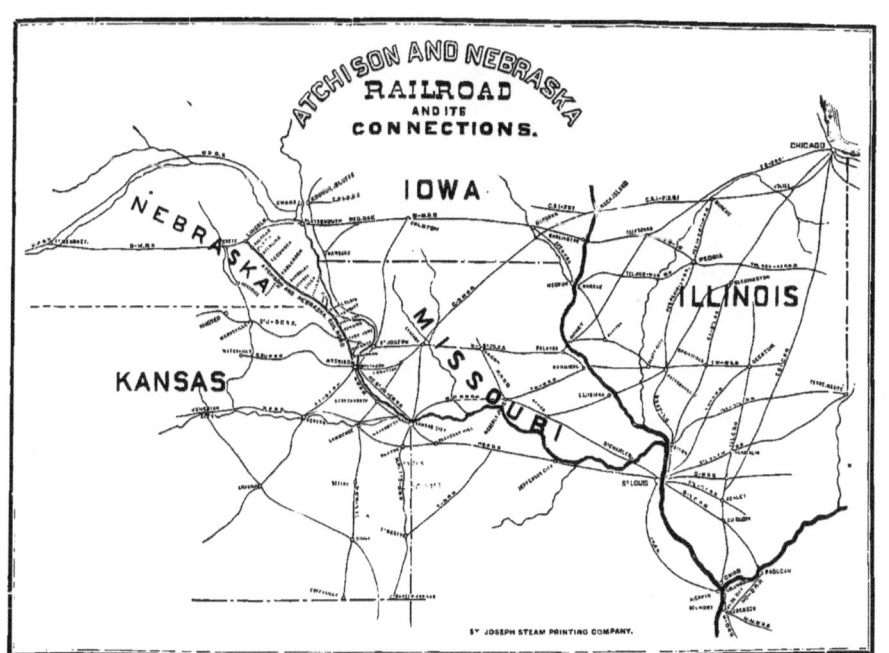

www.ingramcontent.com/pod-product-compliance
Lightning Source LLC
Chambersburg PA
CBHW021135020726
47500CB00003B/1084